camp
CONFIDENTIAL

And the Winner Is . . .

GROSSET & DUNLAP
Published by the Penguin Group
Penguin Group (USA) Inc., 375 Hudson Street, New York,
New York 10014, USA
Penguin Group (Canada), 90 Eglinton Avenue East, Suite 700, Toronto,
Ontario M4P 2Y3, Canada (a division of Pearson Penguin Canada Inc.)
Penguin Books Ltd., 80 Strand, London WC2R 0RL, England
Penguin Group Ireland, 25 St. Stephen's Green, Dublin 2, Ireland
(a division of Penguin Books Ltd.)
Penguin Group (Australia), 250 Camberwell Road, Camberwell, Victoria 3124,
Australia (a division of Pearson Australia Group Pty. Ltd.)
Penguin Books India Pvt. Ltd., 11 Community Centre, Panchsheel Park,
New Delhi—110 017, India
Penguin Group (NZ), 67 Apollo Drive, Rosedale, North Shore 0745,
Auckland, New Zealand (a division of Pearson New Zealand Ltd.)
Penguin Books (South Africa) (Pty.) Ltd., 24 Sturdee Avenue,
Rosebank, Johannesburg 2196, South Africa

Penguin Books Ltd., Registered Offices: 80 Strand, London WC2R 0RL,
England

Cover designed by Ching N. Chan.
Front cover image © Blend Images/Stewart Cohen/Getty Images.

Text copyright © 2007 by Grosset & Dunlap. All rights reserved. Published
by Grosset & Dunlap, a division of Penguin Young Readers Group, 345 Hudson
Street, New York, New York 10014. GROSSET & DUNLAP is a trademark of
Penguin Group (USA) Inc. Printed in the U.S.A.

Library of Congress Cataloging-in-Publication Data is available.

ISBN 978-0-448-44652-3   10 9 8 7 6 5 4 3 2 1

camp CONFIDENTIAL

And the Winner Is . . .

by Melissa J. Morgan

Grosset & Dunlap

Posted by: Natalie
Subject: so sad and so happy

talk about a crazy twenty-four hours. it started last night when logan and i had a really awful, so sad conversation. he told me that he thinks it's too hard doing the long-distance relationship thing. and you know what? i told him i think so, too. it's completely different than at camp lakeview where we saw each other every day. more than once every day. so we're broken up. last night was bad. i just felt so lonely, which is kind of weird because logan and i hardly ever see—make that *saw*—each other, anyway. although we do—make that *did*— e-mail and talk on the phone a lot.

i'm feeling a little better about the logan situation today. a little. what we decided *did* make sense. it *is* hard having a boyfriend you can't even hold hands with once in a while. but it's hard not having a boyfriend at all, too, especially a boyfriend like logan.

then this morning, my dad called me up with

some amazing news that made me forget about logan for a few minutes. here comes the so happy part of this post. are you ready? my dad got nominated for an academy award. can I get a woo-hoo? i told him taking the part in *dark music* would be great for his career. if you haven't seen it, he plays a blind piano player, and the movie totally shows everyone that tad maxwell isn't just about shooting and jumping out of planes and running into fires and all that other action-hero stuff. (not that that stuff isn't cool.)

the best part is I get to go to the oscars!! and all the glam and glitzy after-parties. wait, that's not the best part. the nomination is the best part. yay, dad! but me going to the academy awards is a really good part, right? the oscars are the same week as spring break. i'm going to stay out in hollywood, hanging with my father, the whole vacation. that should keep my mind off logan, right?

love you all! (oh, and tori, get your calendar clear. can't wait to see you!)

natalie

Natalie closed the Camp Lakeview blog. She was so glad it was still going strong. There were times that she really needed her Camp Lakeview girl-friends. And the blog was a lot better than doing a mass e-mail.

I should have asked for opinions on clothes, Natalie thought. She needed to figure out what she was going to bring on her trip. It's not like people in New York didn't care how they looked. They so did. But people in LA *really* cared. They really cared on a normal day. On a night that involved a red carpet, forget about it. And on the ultimate night, or the ultimate red carpet, the one leading into the Kodak Theater where the Academy Awards were held . . . well, that involved teams of prep people. Hair people, makeup people, designers, stylists, nail experts, masseuses, even psychics. Nobody wanted to be one of the worst dressed when *In Touch* and everybody else did the post-Oscars fashion review.

Natalie definitely didn't have anything she wanted to wear to the actual awards ceremony. She had a couple of dresses that were fancy enough, but you couldn't go to the AAs wearing something you'd worn even one time before. Okay, you probably could if you were just the kid of a nominee and not a nominee yourself. But Natalie was far too much of a fashion overachiever to go that route. She was going to be standing next to her father while he got asked over and over how it felt to be nominated for the Best Actor award and who had designed his tux. That called for a new outfit. No, it shouted for one.

To: Tad_Dad
From: NatalieNYC
Re: your reputation

hey, daddums—

 i was thinking. you don't want to be spotted on the red carpet next to a fashion oh-no-you-didn't, do you?

i didn't think so. it just wouldn't be good for your image. that means i need a dress. think you can throw your big movie star—oscar-nominated movie star— weight around and get the girl who won *project runway* this year to let me wear something from her new collection? the collection no one has seen yet.

you remember which one she is, right? her name's lulu, and she's one of those I'm-too-unique-to- need-a-last-name people. she's the one who made the swimsuit out of actual seaweed. don't pretend you don't watch *pr*. I know you do. and not just because it's josie's favorite show and you want to be a good boyfriend.

i'll love you forever if you make it work.

of course, i'll also love you forever if you don't.

love you!

your only daughter

At the same instant Natalie hit Send, she heard the cow moo sound that told her an instant message had arrived. The moo made her laugh—but it also reminded her of Logan. He'd sent her the moo and told her how to make it her IM sound.

She clicked on the message.

<Tori90210>: Finally, someone from Camp Lakeview is coming to LA! I've got my calendar wiped clean! It's my spring break, too, so that means it can be Nat and Tori all the time!

<NatalieNYC>: can't wait.

<Tori90210>: That's it? I don't even get an exclam?!!

<NatalieNYC>: sorry. i started thinking about logan, and it kind of siphoned the excitement out of me for a minute.

<Tori90210>: You want a new boy? There are tons of boys in LA. And I know many of the cutest.

<NatalieNYC>: um, all boys aren't like all other boys, lmho.

<Tori90210>: I know, I know. I was just trying to cheer you up. And even you said it was hard having a BF who lives so far away.

<NatalieNYC>: yeah. sigh.

<Tori90210>: Maybe this will get you smiley again. I've started working on a list of places to go. I know you've been here a bunch to visit your dad, but I just went to this funky place in Koreatown. They have these tiny karaoke rooms that hold about five people. And all the rooms have their own mirror balls. You can't miss it.

<NatalieNYC>: cool. hey, would you be up for the la brea tar pits? i know, i know. they're corny and super touristy. i've never been able to get my dad to take me.

<Tori90210>: I. Worship. The. La. Brea. Tar. Pits. My friends think I'm nuts, but anytime somebody visits from out of town, I always offer to take them there.

When she'd finished making fab LA plans with Tori, Natalie's Logan Loneliness was at a very low level. She started to stand up from her desk chair. She needed to do a thorough closet inspection to see what was Hollywood-worthy.

But first she decided to do a quick check of the camp blog. She wanted to see what her friends had to say about her father's nomination. Maybe at least a few of them had had time to read her post.

Posted by: Valerie
Subject: Woo-hoo

I'm giving up a very loud woo-hoo for Tad Maxwell. WOOOO-HOOOO! That's the coolest, Natalie.

Gotta run. Chelsea, Gaby, and I are still doing volunteer stuff at Home Away From Home. Today we're doing a very cool art project with the kids. We're going to have them lay down on big sheets of butcher paper so we can trace their outlines. Then the kids are going to color themselves in. It was Alyssa's idea. Thanks, Lyss!

Posted by: Grace
Subject: Oscars

Congrats to your dad, Natalie. That is so thrilling. Before I knew he was a nom, I was praying for Mickey Frazier to win. Don't hate me, but he was so awesome in *Nights of Thunder* that I totally forgot to eat my gummy bears! And you know that means something! But now I'm crossing my fingers and toes for your dad to win.

Posted by: Jenna
Subject: Grace

The only reason Grace wanted Mickey Frazier to win in the first place is because she loved the way he looked without his shirt in that scene with the alligator.

Hey, why wasn't that alligator nominated? He was the best thing in that movie.

I have my fingers and toes *and* eyes crossed for your dad, Natalie. Since the gator isn't in the running. ;)

Jenna

Joke of the day: What's the sound of someone laughing his or her head off? Ha, ha, ha—plop!

Posted by: Brynn
Subject: Me, me, me—and Nat's father

Anyone who likes looking at shirtless guys has to come see me in *The Tempest*. I'm Miranda. (Like I haven't told you that already. I know the play is all I talk about.) Anyway, I've never seen anybody but my father, and then there's a shipwreck and I suddenly see all these sailors. Okay, I lied a little. They do wear shirts. But the shirts are all tattered and ripped. Talk about woo-hoo!

I am so psyched to be doing Shakespeare. Shakespeare! You can't call yourself a stage actor if you haven't done the Bard. And the Red Barn Players are awesome. Their plays get reviewed in *The Boston Globe* and everything. The actor who is playing Ferdinand—

Vern Smith—has even been on TV. He was a guest star on *Grey's Anatomy*.

It's actually good that my school doesn't do a play in the spring, huh? Or I'd never have hooked up with the Red Barn group. They are awesome. You have to come see us if you live anywhere near Boston. It's going to be running every weekend for two months, starting in the middle of February.

Okay, enough about me. I can't type anymore, anyway. My hands are too sore from applauding Tad Maxwell's Oscar nomination. That is so absolutely great, wonderful, beautiful . . . and all other good words.

I'll be performing the night of the Oscars, but I'll DVR it and I'll be looking for you on the red carpet, Natalie!

Anon (that's Shakespearean for later),

Brynn

Posted by: Priya
Subject: Already on it!

I already got tickets, Brynn. Jordan and I will be there the first weekend—front row center. Jordan will probably be there every night, just so he can stare at you. I like you lots, but one night of Shakespeare is probably all I can take, so I'm only going once!

P.

Natalie grinned as she read the latest messages on the blog. Then she added one of her own.

Posted by: Natalie
Subject: academy awards

i think we should start an oscar pool. we should each pick the year we think brynn will be nominated. i'm saying year after next. once you have the lead in a shakespearean play, getting an oscar nom is a piece of cake!

okay, enough about brynn. and my dad. let's talk about me! how do you think i should wear my hair for the academy awards? up, down? i'm so excited my brain isn't fully functioning. so help!

nat

"I know you're going to be spending a lot of time poolside, so remember to put on your sunscreen," Natalie's mother said. For the third time that morning.

"I'd never expose myself to photoaging," Nat promised her mom as they moved two steps closer to the ticket counter in NYC's LaGuardia airport. "No UV rays for me."

"My concern was over skin cancer, not you having a few wrinkles when you're my age," her mother answered. "But I don't care why you wear it, just that you do. And no matter what your father says, I want you to get a reasonable amount of sleep. I know it's your vacation, but that doesn't mean you should stay up all night."

"Let me add that to my list," Natalie said. "Number 302, remember to sleep."

Her mom laughed. "Sorry. I guess I have gone a little overboard with the instructions."

They moved up to the front of the line and Natalie handed over her Diane von Furstenberg luggage. Black with just a little bit of pink. So cute. "Gate D fourteen," the woman behind the counter said.

"How many more rules do you think I can lay down before we get to the security checkpoint and I have to let you go?" her mother asked.

"You can talk pretty fast when you want to," Natalie answered as they walked toward the escalator.

"Let me just say this, then," her mother began.

Natalie tried not to roll her eyes. Her mom always had a minor mental breakdown when Nat traveled someplace by herself.

"Have a wonderful time," her mother finished.

A big smile spread across Natalie's face. "Thanks, Mom," she said. She gave her mother a shoulder bump as they stepped onto the escalator. "I know that took major self-control."

"You won't know how much until you put *your* thirteen-year-old daughter on a plane by herself," Natalie's mother joked as they reached the second floor.

"It's not like I haven't flown by myself before," Natalie reminded her. She'd been semi-bicoastal since her parents had gotten divorced when she was four.

They got in the line to go through security. Natalie's mom wouldn't leave her until the last possible moment. Which was about thirty seconds later, because the line was short. Natalie dumped her purse and her carry-on bag on the conveyer belt that led through the X-ray machine, and then gave her mom a hard hug. "Good-bye. I'll call you when I get there," Natalie added as she stepped through the scanner.

"Phone when you get there," her mother called

after her. As if Natalie hadn't said she would one second before.

"I will," Natalie answered over her shoulder as she headed for her gate. She had more than an hour before her flight, so she decided to check out the little gift shop. Maybe she'd find something for her dad. A little congratulatory present for getting nominated.

Maybe a copy of every magazine with his face on the cover, she thought as she passed a row of mags, newspapers, and paperbacks. It would be kind of funny. But funny wasn't exactly what Natalie was going for. Being up for an Academy Award—for the first time—was a big deal.

Nothing on the next row of shelves was right, either. A mini bottle of mouthwash didn't say, "Dad, I'm so proud of you." Neither did a tiny sewing kit, nail clippers, a new toothbrush, or a sample size shampoo and conditioner combo.

Maybe this wasn't the best idea, Nat thought. Then she saw it. The perfect present, over in the corner of the store. A teddy bear in a tuxedo. The bear looked like he was ready to go to the Oscars himself.

Natalie hurried over and took the stuffed animal off the shelf. Her eyes caught on the bear next to it. It was wearing a green T-shirt, just like the one Logan wore all the time at camp. *Maybe I should get it for him,* she thought.

But that was a girlfriend kind of thing. And she wasn't Logan's girlfriend anymore.

Natalie considered buying the bear for herself. She could cuddle it the next time she got a case of the

Logan Lonelies. *No, too pathetic*, she decided. She took the tuxedo-wearing bear up to the register and bought it for her father. She added a Nerds rope for herself. Natalie had gotten addicted to the long, sweet, sticky string with the sour little Nerds candies stuck to it. It was such a weird candy. *Who thinks up stuff like that?* she wondered as she crossed over to the waiting area in front of her gate.

She checked her watch as she dropped down into one of the molded plastic chairs. Still forty-five minutes before the plane was supposed to take off. Which meant boarding in probably twenty. She decided to amuse herself by playing a game she'd made up the last time she was sitting in this airport waiting for a flight to LA. The game was called "Where Ya From?" The point was to decide which of the people around her were native New Yorkers, which were native Californians, and which were from some other state.

Sometimes it was a tough call. Like the guy across from her in the T-shirt that read, *Your Favorite Band Sucks*. The attitude felt very New York to her. But the perfect fading and the perfect fit of the shirt could be either LA or NYC. The sneaks, though—they were a pair of the limited-edition numbers designed by the Kidrobot crew. They were a little more LA. *California born, definitely*, Natalie decided.

"Going home?" Natalie asked the guy. He nodded. *One point for me*, she thought.

By the time first-class boarding was announced, Nat had racked up eleven more points. A twenty-something chick from Denver had completely fooled her.

Natalie had been sure that the Marc Jacobs coat with the row of military-esque gold buttons paired with the wide-brimmed hat had to be worn by a New Yorker. But nope.

Natalie stood up and joined the small group of other first-class passengers. Her dad always bought her a first-class ticket as a special treat. Natalie loved it. The seats were super comfy, and just looking at the desserts got her mouth watering.

But even with the yummy desserts—a hot fudge sundae this time—and a movie that Natalie had been wanting to see, she was eager to get off the plane. She couldn't wait to see her father.

The second the bell dinged and the fasten seat belt sign clicked off, Natalie was on her feet. She snatched her carry-on bag from the overhead compartment and managed to be the first one to say good-bye to the row of flight attendants by the door.

She'd been to LAX so many times that she had no trouble finding the baggage claim area. Her dad should be there somewhere, but she didn't see him. And Tad Maxwell was hard to miss. He was tall, for one thing. And he usually attracted a crowd of noisy fans.

Maybe he's running late, she thought. But her father had a thing about not wanting her hanging out alone in the airport. Natalie did another scan of the area—and spotted a man in a black suit holding a sign that said NATALIE GOODE.

Her father had sent a driver for her.

Ouch.

This has to be an insane time for him, she reminded

herself, walking toward the driver. *He's probably giving a zillion interviews a day, plus photo shoots and talk shows.*

"Hi, I'm Natalie," she told the guy with the sign. He wore his hair short and his sideburns long. And he was really tan, an even golden tan. Spray-on, Natalie decided. It was just too perfect. She pegged him as a guy who drove celebs around, hoping he'd be a celeb himself someday.

"I'm Bingley," he told her. "You can call me Bing. Or Lee. Or Bingley." He grinned, and Natalie had a feeling he used that greeting a lot.

"Where's my dad?" she asked. She sounded like a pouty five-year-old, so she forced herself to smile at Bingley.

"I was just getting to that. Tad's got a meeting with his agent this afternoon, but he wanted me to tell you that tonight he'll take you wherever you want for dinner. And until then, I'm at your service." Bingley gave a little half bow. "Just tell me where you want to go, and we're on our way." He handed her an envelope. "I almost forgot. Fun money from your pops."

"Great," Natalie said. She was glad to hear that she'd gotten the pout out of her voice. "I just have a couple bags." She turned toward the baggage carousel. "That one, the black with pink. And the one that looks just like it, but smaller."

"Diane von Furstenberg. Nice," Bingley commented as he grabbed her suitcases. "So, where to?" he asked as he led the way to the exit.

Where did she want to spend the next few hours? Alone.

Wait. Not necessarily alone! "Give me one sec," Natalie said. She pulled out her cell and called Tori.

"Talk to me," Tori said when she picked up.

"Hey, it's Nat. I just hit the airport. I thought I'd be doing something with my dad this afternoon, but he has meetings and stuff."

"All I'm doing is painting my nails with that water-based stuff you can peel off. It's kind of cool," Tori answered. Her mother was beauty editor at a magazine. Tori always had a ton of beauty products—lots of times before they were even on the shelf. "You know what I'm thinking?" Tori continued.

"What?" Natalie asked.

"I'm thinking I need to smell some tar today," Tori answered.

"Yay! That's perfect. It's exactly what I want to do on my first day in LA," Natalie said. "My dad arranged for a driver. We'll pick you up. Here, tell him where you live."

She handed the phone to Bingley. "I'd like to go to the La Brea Tar Pits. But with a stop on the way to pick up a friend. She's going to give you her address."

"Cool," Bingley answered. "Got it," he said into the cell a moment later.

An hour and fifteen minutes later—LA traffic was hideous—Natalie and Tori were staring at a pool of smelly black tar. It looked like it was boiling, but the bubbles were caused by methane gas being released. The methane gas also caused the smell.

"Brea means 'tar' in Spanish. And la means 'the.' So when you say the La Brea Tar Pits, you're actually saying the the tar tar pits," Tori said.

Natalie laughed. "I think they should sell T-shirts with that on them in the gift shop," she answered.

"Ooooh, gift shop," Tori said.

"Let's hit it," Natalie said. They turned and followed the path to the main building. "It's so bizarre that this tar is oozing out of the ground on the same block as stores and offices and everything," she commented.

"I know. It seems like the pits should be in the middle of Griffith Park at least," Tori answered. She paused to pat one of the giant sloth statues.

"Is it just me, or do giant sloths look kind of like giant prairie dogs?" Natalie asked. "Especially that one that's sitting on its back legs."

"I'm an LA girl. What do I know about prairie dogs?" Tori asked.

"You do go to school and everything, right?" Natalie teased. "Or is it true that you LA girls spend every moment shopping and lying around poolside."

"Watch it. You're half LA girl yourself," Tori said, "even though you aren't blond." She gave her long blond hair a dramatic flip.

Nat remembered how it had kind of bothered her not to be the only Hollywood-connected girl anymore when Tori had arrived at Camp Lakeview. She really hadn't liked Tori at first. But it had turned out to be really fun having a friend who knew LA even better than Natalie did herself.

"Let's spend the guilt money my dad had the driver give me," Natalie suggested as they walked into the cool, dim museum. She pulled the envelope out of her purse and opened it. "Here. Twenty-five for you. Twenty-five for me."

"My parents gave me cash, too," Tori protested.

"Save it. My dad would want to treat you since I'm here on vacay," Natalie answered. "Besides, I used some of my own money to buy him a present. This adorable teddy bear wearing a tux."

"Like he's ready to go to the Academy Awards," Tori said, immediately getting the connection.

"Uh-huh. I almost bought myself a bear at the same time. There was this one that so reminded me of Logan," Natalie admitted. She led the way into the gift shop.

"The breakup really was hard for you, wasn't it?" Tori asked.

"Yeah. I miss him. Even though we couldn't see each other in person, we used to IM all the time. And we talked on the phone every couple days," Natalie explained. She paused in front of one of the glass cases that circled the center of the store, but her mind was on Logan, not the jewelry and pottery on display.

"I'm making it my mission to keep your brain off Logan while you're here. You're thinking about him right now, I can tell," Tori said. "We need . . ." She glanced around the shop. "Postcards!" she exclaimed. "We're going to buy postcards for every girl we know at camp. Then we're going to go over to the Coffee Bean and Tea Leaf and flirt with the counter guys. Well, you'll flirt. I'll just look while simultaneously keeping in mind that I already have my very own hottie of a boyfriend. Plus, Adam Brody goes there practically every day for a latte, according to *LAglitz*. So we can flirt with him, too."

"Good idea!" Natalie exclaimed. They hurried over to the tall rack of postcards. "I think Alyssa would like any of the ones with the sculptures on them. She's such an art girl."

"And Priya and Jenna would probably want to see the actual bones," Tori added.

"I'm going to buy one for my dad, too," Natalie decided. "To show him all the fun he missed out on."

By the time they'd written all their post-cards—and done some flirting with the counter guys *and* giggled at Adam Brody as he bought a latte—it was time to head home. Natalie couldn't wait to tell her dad about all the fun she'd had with Tori. She was out of the car almost before Bingley pulled to a stop in her father's driveway. "Thanks!" she called over her shoulder.

She didn't bother rooting around in her purse to find her key. She just pounded on the door with both hands. "Dad, I'm back!" she cried. "Get out here!"

There was no answer. No sound of feet rushing toward the door.

Maybe he's out by the pool. Or working out in the gym with his music cranked up, Natalie thought. She dug out her key and opened the door. The huge house was silent. It felt empty.

She hurried into the kitchen. She and her father always left notes for each other stuck to the fridge with Monopoly magnets. When she was little, they had played Monopoly every time they saw each other.

Natalie spotted an index card under one of the

magnets. She pulled it down and read the message in her father's neat, all caps printing. SU SCHEDULED A PHOTO SHOOT FOR TONITE. SORRY! RAIN CHECK? TONS OF FOOD IN FRIDGE. OR ORDER SOMETHING. MENUS ON TABLE.

Natalie let out a sigh that felt like it had started at the tips of her toenails. Then she pulled the teddy bear out of its bag. "I guess it's just you and me tonight, huh?"

chapter

THREE

Natalie opened her eyes at five A.M. the next morning. She never woke up that early. She figured it was because her body was still on NYC time. It was already eight there.

Plus, she was really excited to see her dad. He was probably still asleep. But he wouldn't want to be if he knew she was up. She leaped out of bed and tromped over to the bathroom that adjoined her room, trying to make as much noise as possible. To give her dad a hint. She loudly shut the door behind her. To give her dad another hint. He was a pretty heavy sleeper. He snored and everything.

Natalie washed her face, brushed her teeth, then put on her new brand-new La Brea Tar Pits T-shirt and her favorite jeans, the pair that she'd cut to capri length. Then she headed for the kitchen. Before she'd taken three steps, her dad had her in a big hug. He swung her off the ground, spun her in a circle, and then set her back on her feet. "Natalie-boo! I'm so happy you're here."

"Me too," Natalie said.

"Did you remember to call your mom last

night to let her know you arrived okay?" he asked as they walked to the kitchen together.

"If I didn't, she'd already be pounding on your door," Natalie joked.

"True," her dad answered.

"Hey, did you see the present I got you?" Natalie pointed to the stuffed bear she'd left sitting in her dad's usual chair at the kitchen table.

"I saw it, but I didn't know it was for me." He picked up the bear and looked it over.

"It's a happy-Oscar-nomination gift," Natalie explained.

"Thanks, sweetie," he said.

"I'm so proud of you. An Oscar nomination. That's huge! And you already won the People's Choice Award," Natalie reminded him.

"The Oscar *is* kinda huge, isn't it?" Her dad ran his fingers through his hair. "You know, I've been really lucky. I got that part in *Big Bad City* right out of drama school. It took off, and I've been working ever since. But pretty much the same kinds of parts."

"I know. *Dark Music* is the first movie you didn't need a stuntman for," Natalie answered.

"It's like, for the first time, people around town are looking at me and seeing a real actor, somebody who really did go to drama school, not just an action movie guy," her dad said. He leaned close to Natalie. "Confession?" he whispered in her ear. "I know it's supposed to be an honor just to be nominated and everything, but I really want to win."

"You're going to!" Natalie exclaimed. "You were

awesome in *Dark Music*. All my friends thought so. They're *all* rooting for you."

Her father laughed. "Then it's a lock." He grabbed a bottle of pomegranate-blueberry juice out of the fridge. "Want a glass? It's loaded with antioxidants," he told her.

"Sure." Natalie grabbed a seat at the table. "And a muffin, please. You did get my favorite lemon poppy seed ones from Trader Joe's, right? And when I say you, I mean Ms. Davis." Ms. Davis was her dad's housekeeper. He had a crew of people. Su, his publicist. Heath, his agent. Mary, his personal trainer. Lee, his personal assistant. Sunny, his lawyer. And Allis, his lawyer.

"Of course. Ms. Davis knows all the things you like. The whole kitchen is stocked," her father answered. He set the juice and a muffin down in front of her.

"You're just having juice?" she asked as he sat down. Her dad usually had a big bowl of Cocoa Puffs every morning, the only junk food he allowed himself. Semi-junk food. It *was* vitamin enriched, as he liked to remind her.

"I have a photo shoot for *Vanity Fair* in an hour. They want a picture of all the Best Actor nominees together. I might end up standing next to Mickey Frazier. I don't want to be bloated. Have you seen that guy with his shirt off?" he joked. Half joked.

"Oh." Natalie had thought she'd have her dad to herself today. "I think I'll get in some pool time. Then you can take me to the movies at the Cinerama Dome. You know I can't come to LA without doing the Dome."

"I can't today, Nat. I have to tape my segment of the Barbara Walters special. Not that I wouldn't rather hang with you than Babs," her father said. "I knew when I invited you out for the week that I'd have a lot of obligations. But I really didn't realize how many. I'm sorry."

Natalie forced a smile. She knew what a huge deal it was for her dad to have been nominated for an Oscar, and she wasn't going to do anything to spoil it for him. "No worries," she said. "Tori—you know, my Camp Lakeview friend—and I have tons of plans. She's on spring break, too. We had an awesome time at the tar pits yesterday. Maybe we'll hit Pink's for lunch. It turns out that she's a Pink's freak just like me."

"That's great! Bingley will take you two wherever you want to go. Have him drive you to Pink's if you want. Just keep the hot dog consumption under control. No more than ten, agreed?"

Natalie giggled. "Agreed."

"Hey, and how about inviting Tori to go to the Oscars with us? I have one extra ticket. Josie was going to use it, but she's on location in Santa Fe for the next month," her father offered.

"Really? Really, really, really?" Natalie could hardly believe it.

"Really," her dad answered.

"Tori's going to die!" Natalie exclaimed. "I'm going to have to give her CPR so she'll be able to go with us."

▲ ▲ ▲

Tori shook her head at her boyfriend, Michael.

"What? I got all perfects!" he said, pointing to

his Dance Dance Revolution score on the big plasma screen.

"But you dance like a zombie," Tori told him. She stood up and did a little imitation of Michael playing DDR, her feet barely lifting off the floor, arms flopping limply at her sides.

"Really? I look that hot?" Michael joked.

Tori laughed. Michael was always making her laugh. "Yeah, you make a completely hot zombie," she told him. Seriously, he was so cute with his long emo bangs and his golden brown eyes.

He started to shuffle toward her, making weird grunting sounds, his eyes rolled up in his head. Tori backed away slowly. "Got to say, your hotness level is going down." He grabbed her.

"Brains. Need brains," he grunted as he pretended he was about to take a bite out of her head.

"Way down!" Tori warned him. The sound of a meowing kitten came faintly from her bedroom. "That's my cell," she said. She gave Michael a gentle push. "Be right back."

She hurried into her room and grabbed her cell. The kitty sound meant she had a text message. She brought it up.

scored you a tic to the oscars!! (!!!!!!) so what are you wearing? xxoo nat

Tori let out a squeal loud enough to be heard in space. She was going to the Academy Awards! Big, big exclam.

"What?" Michael exclaimed, bursting in.

"I am going to the Oscars! My dad can't even get tickets and he's the lawyer for practically half the nominees. And I'm going! Natalie's dad is giving me a ticket!" Tori cried. "I need to get a haircut. And a mani-pedi. And a spray tan. I bet Dane is totally booked. I'll have to do some serious begging."

"I guess this means you won't be going to Isley's Oscar party with me," Michael said.

"Oh." Tori's smile drooped. "I completely forgot . . ."

"It's okay," Michael said. "I know you live for the Academy Awards."

"You're the best," Tori told him.

"Now at least I won't have to sit in front of the TV the whole party," Michael continued. "And we can do lots of other stuff during vacation."

"Um . . ." Tori hesitated.

"Um what?" Michael asked, his eyes narrowing.

"Um, I kind of told Natalie that I'd clear my calendar for the week," Tori answered. "It's just that we hardly ever see each other except in the summer."

"I hardly ever see you, either," Michael complained. "We only have one class together, and I have basketball practice, and you have choir. Plus we both have twelve tons of homework."

"It's not like we won't spend any time together over vacay," Tori promised him. "Natalie's going to be hanging with her dad a lot of the time. It'll be all good."

"Okay," Michael said. But he didn't sound that happy about it.

Brynn couldn't take her eyes off her friend Rosemary as she began Brynn's favorite part in the whole play.

"Full fathoms five thy father lies," Rosemary, as the spirit Ariel, sang to Vern, the boy who was playing Ferdinand in the Red Barn Players' version of *The Tempest*. Rosemary, Vern, and Brynn were the only teenagers in the cast.

The words of the song were just so beautiful. "Nothing of him that doth fade / But doth suffer a sea-change / Into something rich and strange," Brynn sang softly under her breath along with Rosemary.

It's your own lines you should be practicing, Brynn told herself. This rehearsal was off book. That meant everybody was supposed to have every bit of their part memorized.

And she thought she did. She was pretty sure. It was just that Jordan had been IMing her the whole time she was going over her lines last night. He always found the most outrageous things to send her. Like a maze where if you made a mistake, that creepy kid from *The Grudge* popped up on the screen and screeched at you. Or this YouTube clip of a dancing cockroach that was so gross. And cool.

Just thinking about the cockroach made her laugh. And it really wasn't a part in the play anybody should be laughing at. Ariel was trying to make Ferdinand believe that his father had drowned.

Knowing she shouldn't laugh made Brynn laugh

harder. It was this awful thing that happened to her sometimes. The director, Ms. Milligan, shot her an annoyed glance. She expected everyone in the cast to be professional, and laughing at an inappropriate moment was definitely not professional behavior.

Brynn's cheeks flushed. She had to get control of herself. She bit down on the inside of her cheek—a good, hard chomp—until the desire to cackle passed. Then she opened her script to the scene she and Vern would be doing later. Brynn had a couple of long speeches in it, and she wasn't as comfortable with them as she wanted to be.

She slumped down in her seat and brought the script close to her face, trying to block out everything but the words. "I do not know / One of my sex, no woman's face remember / Save from my glass mine own; nor have I seen / More that I may call men than you, good friend," she murmured to herself.

Then Brynn paused to think about what the words really meant. It helped her remember them, and it really helped her bring emotion to the scene. Ferdinand had just given Miranda a compliment, more like a paragraph of compliments, about how beautiful she was. Then Miranda explains to him that she has never seen another woman. She's only seen her own face. And she hasn't seen any man other than Ferdinand, except her father.

Brynn tried to imagine what it would be like to see Vern/Ferdinand if she'd never seen another human besides her father. Vern was one of the best-looking guys Brynn had ever laid eyes on. He had wheat-colored hair, and the most beautiful smoky blue eyes. Sometimes when he was in a serious mood, which he was a lot of the time, they'd look almost gray.

But would Miranda even know how handsome Ferdinand was? Did you need to compare someone to other people to realize they were exceptional? Or would anyone, even a girl who had lived on an almost deserted island her whole life, instantly see the beauty of his eyes? And his perfectly shaped mouth? And—

"Hey!" a voice said in her ear.

Brynn lowered her script—and saw Jordan sliding into the seat next to hers at the back of the theater.

"You're not really supposed to be here," she whispered.

"It's nice to see you, too," Jordan joked.

Brynn glanced around the theater. She figured no one would notice one extra person. Most of the cast was scattered throughout the seats. She pressed her finger against her lips to tell him they had to be quiet. "Sorry," she answered softly. "I'm just stressed. I'm not sure I have all my lines down for the scene I have to do today. Last time we rehearsed it, I had to keep looking at my script, even though I was supposed to have my part memorized. Today the director isn't even allowing us to hold the scripts."

"You'll be great," Jordan whispered.

"I'll be great if I know my lines. Just let me read over them a few times, okay?" Brynn asked.

"Sure," Jordan answered. "I'll just watch the Shakespeare. You know how I do love it."

Brynn snorted, then brought her script up in

front of her face. "I do not know / One of my sex, no woman's face remember / Save from my glass," she began to read.

"I found this cool game online last night," Jordan whispered. "I'm going to send you a link."

"Cool. But studying here," Brynn answered without lowering the script.

"I know, I know. I just wanted to tell you, so you could remind me if I forgot to send it," Jordan said.

Brynn focused her attention on her lines. She'd highlighted them in pink.

"It's called Kingdom of Loathing," Jordan added a moment later.

How could Brynn not ask? She lowered her script. "Kingdom of Loathing?"

"Yeah. It's so cool. You can play as a Pastamancer, a Turtle Tamer, a Disco Bandit—"

"I don't even have to hear any more. I'm going to be a Disco Bandit," Brynn told him. How did Jordan do it? He found all the coolest stuff online.

"Excellent choice. Here's the deal." Jordan laid out the game for her, giving her the strategy he'd come up with and the tips he'd read on the player forum.

"All right, people," Ms. Milligan called out, interrupting him. "We're going to move on to Act three, Scene one. I hate to skip around so much, but with our Prospero home sick, it's necessary."

"That's me," Brynn told Jordan. "Are you sure you want to hang here? I know it's not that exciting to watch rehearsals."

"But eating ice cream is. And that's what we're

36

going to do as soon as you get your lunch break," Jordan said. "I still can't believe you have to spend so much of vacation rehearsing."

"The play opens—" Brynn began.

"This is you, Brynn," Ms. Milligan reminded her.

"Got to go," Brynn said. She stood up, squeezed past Jordan, and hurried to the spot where she would make her entrance stage left. Vern was already in place for the opening of the scene.

"I'll read Prospero's asides, since Jim isn't with us," Ms. Milligan said. "It shouldn't affect you too much since your characters aren't supposed to realize he's watching you."

Brynn and Vern nodded. Then Vern began pretending to make a pile of logs while he gave his opening lines. He didn't miss a single word, as far as Brynn could tell. He was such a total pro. Her heart started to beat faster. *Don't let me mess up,* she thought as she joined Vern onstage. She hadn't even gotten to read through her part one time. Thanks to Jordan and all that Kingdom of Loathing talk. Why hadn't she told him to just be quiet?

Answer? Jordan was just too much fun.

She got through her first speech—the one about how she hated to see Vern working so hard on her father's orders—without a problem. The words came easily out of her mouth, like she was talking to Rosemary or Jordan.

With each moment, she felt more and more like Miranda. When she looked at Vern/Ferdinand, she felt herself melt a little, her knees going a little gooey the way Miranda's would. All these feelings were so new to Miranda, and Brynn's voice got a little breathy as she spoke to the beautiful boy.

Is it weird for Jordan to see me looking at another guy this way? The thought snaked through Brynn's mind, distracting her as she began her "I do not know" speech. She made it to the third line, then blanked. She knew the line had something to do with looking in the mirror, but the correct phrase wouldn't come to her. She stammered to a stop.

"You have to keep going, Brynn," Ms. Milligan instructed. "We go into previews this weekend. If you forget your lines in front of an audience, you can't just stand there in silence. That is completely unacceptable. You must find a way through the scene."

"No woman's face remember," Brynn said, going back to the previous line, hoping that would make the next one come to her. It didn't. "Except from mine mirror," she said, knowing the words were wrong. She stumbled her way through the rest of the speech, feeling as if she was getting more of it wrong than right.

Vern had a longish speech after that. *Get a grip*, Brynn ordered herself as he spoke. *Get a grip, get a grip, get a grip.* She wasn't responding to Vern/Ferdinand's words at all. She was giving him nothing as an actress. But her brain was too full of panic for her to focus on the scene.

She managed to get out her one line of response to what Vern/Ferdinand had said. Then he had a bunch of lines. She remembered her two-line response. Then it was her/Miranda's turn to make a speech. Ten lines. It didn't take more than a minute to speak ten lines. But that minute felt like a solid year in hell to Brynn. Sweat actually started popping out along her hairline as she fought her way through the tongue-twisting Shakespearean phrases.

Finally, the scene was done.

"We have already sold out more than half the performances we're scheduled to give," Ms. Milligan said. "I have to say, I would be ashamed to take money for what I just saw." She turned to look at Vern. "Not from you. I respect the way you stayed in character all the way through that charade."

Ms. Milligan returned her gaze to Brynn. "I hesitated to cast teenagers in this production. But I thought a young Ferdinand and Miranda added so much. And I thought a teen would be an interesting choice for Ariel." She shook her head. "You disappoint me, Brynn. I thought you were mature enough to be professional."

"I'm sorry. I'll . . . I'll do better," Brynn promised, her voice shaking. She'd never had a moment like that onstage before. And she'd been in dozens of plays.

Ms. Milligan gave a sharp nod. "Moving on. Trinculo, Caliban, Stefano, and Ariel, next scene."

Brynn couldn't wait to get off the stage. Another first. She rushed into the wings, Vern right behind her.

"You better pull it together, Brynn," he snapped. "You're not in a high school play. We're going to get reviewed in the *Globe*. And we're all going to be humiliated if you lose it the way you just did. You might not care about your acting career, but I care about mine."

He didn't give her time to answer, just turned and strode away.

Brynn felt her heart sink down into her stomach. Vern was right. Ms. Milligan was right. She could ruin the show. She *would* ruin the entire show if she didn't make sure she knew every single word of her part before the weekend.

chapter

FOUR

"Nat! Back here," Tori called as she opened the gate leading to the side patio of her house. "I have the most amazing news," she cried as soon as Natalie stepped inside.

"What?" Natalie asked as she joined her friend.

"We're going to the Academy Awards!" Tori squealed.

Natalie laughed. "How extremely cool is that! I'm so excited that you're coming with me. It's going to be way more fun with you there."

"Of course it is. I rock," Tori joked. "So, we're going in a limo, right?"

"Is there another way to get to the Oscars?" Natalie asked.

Tori pretended to think about it. "That would be no."

"And afterward, we're going to parties, parties, and then more parties. The Governor's Ball first, then what do you think? Should we go to the *Vanity Fair* one next? Or the one Elton John gives? Or—"

"Uh, hello. Boyfriend here."

Natalie turned toward the voice and saw a tall guy with curly blond hair and deep blue eyes.

"Oops, sorry. That's Michael. And, yes, he's my boyfriend," Tori said.

"Hi," Natalie said. "I'm—"

"I know who you are. You're the girl who Tori dumped me for," Michael joked as he handed her a glass.

"Wait. What?" Natalie asked.

"Tori told me she has no time for me this week because her fabulous friend Natalie is in town," Michael explained. "She allowed me to stay because she needed somebody to serve drinks. I made Arnold Palmers." He nodded to the tray of lemonade/iced tea blends on the patio table. "Now that my work is done, I probably have to leave."

"That's right. We'll call you if we need refills," Tori teased. She smiled at Nat. "I wanted you two to meet each other. But we're definitely not letting Michael go out with us. You should hear him whine if he gets within ten feet of a shoe store. And I definitely need new shoes for the Oscars. I need new everything."

"Unfair," Michael protested. "I only whine, as you call it, because you get sucked into every single shoe store you pass, even if we're late for a movie or something."

"Sounds good to me," Natalie answered.

"See? That's why I had to clear my calendar to hang with Natalie. She understands me," Tori told Michael.

Michael drained his glass with two long gulps. "Okay, message received. I'm out."

"Wait. Why can't the three of us do something together?" Natalie suggested. It didn't seem fair to hog Tori for the whole vacation. "There has to be something in this town we can all agree on."

"Something that doesn't involve shoes?" Michael asked hopefully.

"Something we like to do that doesn't involve shoes. Let's think," Natalie said to Tori.

Tori tilted her head to the side. "Hmmm." She tilted her head to the other side, furrowing her brow. "Hmmm." She winked at Natalie. "How about . . . the Santa Monica Pier?" she finally asked.

"Pier. You said pier. Not promenade, right?" Michael asked.

Natalie laughed. She had been to the Santa Monica Pier and the Santa Monica Promenade. Pier— no shoe stores. Promenade—shoe stores aplenty. "She said pier. I heard her," she reassured Michael.

Michael looked over at Tori. "Excellent. How about if I call Reed and see if he wants to go?"

"Reed is one of Michael's cooler friends," Tori explained to Natalie.

"He's way cooler than me," Michael said.

"Then he should definitely come," Natalie answered. "I have a car and driver for the day. We can have him pick up your friend and then take us to the pier."

Michael pulled out his cell. "Sounds like a plan."

▲ ▲ ▲

Natalie took a deep breath of ocean air as she, Tori, Michael, and Reed walked down the pier. She loved the smell of the sea. Her favorite bath bomb was called Big Blue, and it turned the tub into a mini-ocean, complete with bits of seaweed and the amazing smell.

Reed took a deep breath, too. "Remember that *Seinfeld* episode where Kramer wanted to make a perfume that smelled like the ocean? I would definitely buy that."

Tori rolled her eyes. "Reed, no one but you watches *Seinfeld*."

"Somebody has to. It's on about three times a day," Reed answered.

"Those somebodys—old people," Michael explained.

Reed shrugged. "I mostly like it because it's set in New York," he explained. "That's where I'm from originally. I'm still kind of from there. At least the vacations when it's my mom's turn to have me. My parents are divorced," he added.

"Mine too. I'm like the opposite of you," Natalie said. "I live with my mom in New York most of the time. But I come out here on a lot of vacations to see my dad."

"So what first?" Michael asked. "Although I already know what the fish head will say."

"Fish head?" Natalie repeated.

"Reed," Tori explained. "He's really into oceanography. He always wants to go to the aquarium."

"I've been here a bunch of times, and I didn't even know there was an aquarium," Natalie said.

"It's right under the carousel," Reed told her. "It's insane. If you haven't seen it, you have to go."

"Sounds fun," Natalie answered.

"Why don't you two go?" Tori asked. "I have to ride the Plunge at least five times."

"Let's meet up for lunch in an hour and a half," Michael said. "At the place with the good french fries."

"You know which place that is?" Natalie asked Reed.

"Of course. One time Michael and I did a compare and contrast of all the french fries on the pier. We found the ones that are the perfect combo of crunchy, salty, and greasy."

"Okay, then. We'll see you there in a while," Nat told Tori.

"Have fun with the fishies," Tori called as she and Michael started toward the rides. Her tone made it clear that she wasn't entirely sure fun and fish could actually be had together.

"I think Tori's only interested in fish when it's stuffed into a sushi roll," Reed commented.

Natalie laughed as they took the stairs leading to the beach. Tori was right. Reed was cool.

"So where first?" she asked when they walked into the aquarium.

"I usually start with the shark and stingray tank," Reed said. "Just so you know, touching them is not allowed."

"But I wanted to pet a shark," Natalie protested

playfully. She stopped in front of the low tank and stared into the water.

"They get scared really easily," Reed explained.

Natalie stepped back as a mottled purple head broke free of the water. Its eyes looked demonic. They were this freaky shade of yellow-brown. "Seriously? I know that thing is small. But it looks like it wants to eat my face off with its million tiny little teeth."

"It's dangerous to smaller fish—that's what it eats. But it's definitely not a threat to people. It's a swell shark. It's called that because it can pump water into its stomach and make its body swell up," Reed told her.

"Why would it want to do that?" Natalie asked. "Doesn't it know it lives in LA? Everybody wants to be thin here."

Reed laughed. "It makes it harder to pull it out from between rocks. Also, it makes it tougher for bigger fish to swallow it."

"You really do like this stuff, don't you?" Natalie asked.

"Yeah. I started coming here a lot around the time my parents decided to split. My mom really hated it in LA. And my dad was starting to get a lot of directing jobs out here. They were always screaming at each other." Reed shrugged. "This place is always quiet. And it's educational, so my parents were always okay with me coming here."

"I could have used a place like this when my parents were getting a divorce," Natalie admitted. There was something so calm about the life going on in the tanks. Hanging in the aquarium with Reed was a great way to spend time. Since her dad's schedule was too crazed to fit her in.

△ △ △

"Do you want me to eat this whole banana split by myself?" Jordan asked Brynn. "Because I have the stomach capacity, and I'm not afraid to use it."

Brynn took a spoonful of the strawberry side of the split. Her favorite. But she didn't even register tasting it before she swallowed. She pushed the glass dish closer to Jordan. "Go for it," she told him.

"You're really upset about forgetting your lines, aren't you?" His green eyes were locked on her face.

Duh, you think? Brynn thought. Immediately, she felt bad. Jordan was being sympathetic. It wasn't his fault she'd messed up so badly at rehearsal. She could have stopped IMing him any time she wanted to last night. He would have understood that she needed time to work on her part.

"You heard what Ms. Milligan said to me," Brynn answered. "And Vern . . ." She shook her head.

"Who's Vern?" Jordan asked.

"He's the guy who plays Ferdinand," she explained.

"The one you're supposed to be in love with." Jordan gave the ice cream a stir with his spoon. It was getting soupy because they'd been taking so long to eat it.

"Miranda, not me, but yeah," Brynn said. "He said that I was going to humiliate everyone in the show if I didn't get it together. I don't know how I'm even going to be able to look at him when we rehearse our next scene together."

"Do you like him or something?" Jordan asked, his voice harsh.

"What? No," Brynn answered. She started to tear her napkin into little pieces.

"You care an awful lot about what he thinks of you," Jordan commented.

"Because . . . because I care about what everyone in the cast thinks. If I mess up during a performance, the way I just did at rehearsal, I'll wreck the whole play for all of them," Brynn explained.

Jordan nodded. Then he grabbed a straw, stuck it into the melting ice cream split, and sucked some up with a loud slurp.

Brynn giggled. Jordan could almost always make her laugh. He was the best.

"It will be okay," she said. "I'm just going to practice my lines every second of every day. I'm going to have my part down ice cold before the weekend."

"Yeah, you should be working on your lines the rest of the vacation, whenever we're not doing something." Jordan slurped up some more ice cream.

But Brynn needed every second, every single second that she wasn't onstage at a rehearsal, to practice her part. She was going to brush her teeth with the script in one hand. She was going to eat with it propped in front of her. She'd even sleep with it under her pillow, so it could get into her dreams.

How was she supposed to find time to do anything with Jordan?

Disappointment flooded through her as she answered her own question. She wasn't going to get any more Jordan time until the play was over. Even when she had her lines down and there were no more rehearsals, she'd be performing six nights a week, plus doing a matinee on Saturday. She'd have to use every free second just to get her homework done. Every single teacher she had gave a ton.

That meant it would be months before she and Jordan could get together.

▲ ▲ ▲

"I think I see Reed and Nat," Tori said to Michael as she peered out at the beach from their Ferris wheel car.

"Yep, that's them," Michael agreed.

"Good call asking Reed to come with us." Tori pulled a strand of hair off her mouth. It had gotten stuck in her lip gloss as the Ferris wheel spun through the sky. "Natalie just broke up with this guy from camp. She was really bummed about it. I think Reed's making her feel better."

And Tori was happy about that. She was. She just wished . . . she couldn't help wishing she and Natalie had been able to spend more of the day together. It was cool when Reed and Nat went off to the aquarium together. Tori had wanted them to do that. Seeing them together, she could tell Reed was helping with the Logan sitch.

But then they'd ended up eating lunch separately, too. Michael had decided he had to have clams, and

Reed and Nat weren't in the mood after staring at all the sea creatures in the aquarium. They'd gone to the pizza place.

Then Michael had wanted to go on the Ferris wheel, and Natalie had really wanted to get some beach time in, which made sense, because she didn't live practically on top of the beach the way the rest of them did. And Tori hadn't felt like she could say no to Michael since he'd gone on her favorite ride with her a bunch of times. The way the day had turned out, Natalie and Tori might as well still have been three thousand miles apart.

"And this way we got to do some stuff together," Michael commented. "Even though you're still going to ditch me for the rest of the week."

"Come on, Michael. You know I'm just trying to get in my Nat time while I can. I'll make it up to you." She snuggled closer to him. "It was fun today. Thanks for helping me break my record for consecutive rides on the Plunge," Tori said.

"I can't believe you actually like that ride. It's one step up from the plane ride in Kiddie Cove," Michael teased.

"Not true," Tori protested. "The Plunge—"

She was interrupted by a meow coming from inside her purse. "I'm getting a text message," she told Michael. She pulled out her cell and checked the screen.

How did Tori-Nat day go? Tons o' fun? Wish I was with.
Val

How was she supposed to answer Valerie? It was almost time to head home, and Tori and Natalie had hardly spent any time together. Tori did some quick mental math. Since they'd arrived at the pier, she and Natalie had spent a total of approximately sixteen minutes together.

Sixteen minutes wasn't a ton o' anything. Definitely not tons o' Natalie and Tori having fun together.

chapter
FIVE

Gr8 time yest. Can I C U some more? Reed

Natalie grinned as she read Reed's message a second time. Then she snapped her cell closed, stuck it in her pocket, and trotted downstairs. She smelled what she was pretty sure were blueberry pancakes. Her dad knew they were her favorite. He was probably already at the kitchen table, waiting to have breakfast with her.

Wrong. He was at the dining room table. And he wasn't waiting to have breakfast with her. He was in the middle of having breakfast with Su, Heath, Allis, Sunny, and Lee. The only missing member of his team was Mary, but it would be hard for him to work out with his trainer while strategizing about his career with the others.

"Hey, babe," her dad called. "I had Ms. Davis make your favorite pancakes."

"None for your breakfast meeting?" Natalie asked, scanning the table. It looked like everyone was doing fruit juice and coffee only.

"No time," Su said. "Plus none of us have

the metabolism for pancakes anymore." She smiled at Natalie. "Enjoy your youth!"

"No time?" Natalie repeated. She managed to stop herself from adding the word "again."

"Your dad has a rehearsal in less than an hour," Heath explained. "He's one of the presenters at the show, so he has to practice his witty introduction to the movies nominated for Best Sound Editing."

"Sorry, Nat," her father said. "I thought it was tomorrow. I'm having a hard time keeping my schedule straight."

"Speaking of your schedule," Lee said, "we need to leave."

"We can go over your new contract in the car," said Allis.

"And remember, you're doing Oprah's *Live in LA* show," Su chimed in.

"Sorry," her father said to Natalie again. "I'll make it up to you. I promise."

"It's okay. I knew you'd be busy this week," she answered, trying to mean it. "I guess I better get to my pancakes before they get cold."

"Bingley's around if you want to go anywhere. I gave him some cash for you," her father called after her. "Have a great day!"

Reed's text message popped into her head as Natalie sat down at the kitchen table. He'd said he had a great time with her yesterday. Maybe he'd be up for getting together today. He probably knew what it was like to visit one of your parents and have them totally tied up with work.

Natalie pulled out her cell and found his number, then hit Send. Ms. Davis set a plate full of pancakes and a pitcher of warm blueberry syrup in front of her.

"Thanks," she said.

"For what?" Reed asked in her ear. "And who is this?"

Natalie laughed. "It's me. Nat. I didn't think you'd picked up yet. I was saying thanks to someone else."

"So what's up?" Reed said.

"Um, you wanted to know if we could get together again. And I wanted to know if today would—" Natalie began.

"Absolutely," Reed interrupted.

"Great. My dad is busy for pretty much ever," she told him. "I know everything he's doing is important, but when I'm in LA—"

"You want to hang with him," Reed interrupted again. "I get that. When I'm in New York, I think my mom should be available 24/7. Unless I have plans with my friends."

"Exactly!" Natalie exclaimed. Reed really got the divorced parent thing. Her father only got to see her in person a few times a year. It hurt that he hadn't made her his absolute top priority. Even though she understood how important his Oscar nomination was and how many responsibilities he had this week.

"I know exactly where we should go," Reed said. "Do you have your driver again today?"

"Uh-huh," Natalie answered.

"Tell him to take you to Hollywood and Ivar. I'll meet you at the subway station on the corner," Reed told her.

"We can pick you up," Natalie said.

"No, I like the subway. It makes me feel like I'm in Manhattan," Reed answered. "I'm leaving in five. See you there."

Natalie tried to leave in five, but guys didn't have as much to do before they went out. No makeup. Hardly any hair care. Still, even with all her girl activities, she and Bingley were on the road eleven minutes after she hung up with Reed.

She thought she might beat him to their meeting place anyway, since she was going by car and he was going by subway. But Reed was leaning against the bright red car statue when Bingley stopped at the corner.

"I'll take the car into that lot," Bingley said. "Just call on my cell when you want me."

"Thanks, Bing!" Natalie called as she climbed out onto the sidewalk. Reed headed over to meet her. "So where are we going?" she asked him.

"It's a surprise," he said.

"Do we need the car?" Natalie asked. "Bing's parking it right over there."

"No, we're going to do something that most Los Angelinos never do—walk," Reed told her. "Come on." He started down the sidewalk, Natalie by his side. "It's just about a block away."

Natalie scanned the souvenir shops that ran on both sides of the street, trying to figure out where Reed was taking her. This stretch of Hollywood Boulevard was pretty touristy—probably because it was the section where all the stars had their stars on the sidewalk.

"Why do I feel like I'm missing something?" Natalie asked as they walked.

"I don't know. Why?" Reed asked.

"My cell. That's it," Natalie realized. "I always have it."

"You probably just left it in the car. I have mine if you need one," Reed said. "Okay, we're here." Reed stopped next to a Blimpies sandwich place.

"I just scarfed down a protein bar," Natalie told him, feeling a little confused. "But if you're hungry . . ."

"Not that place. Look down," Reed instructed.

Natalie did—and realized she was standing on her father's star. The name TAD MAXWELL was written in gold letters in the center of a pale pink star.

"It sounded like you were really wishing you could spend some time with your dad, so—" Reed pointed at the star.

"You're a goofball," Natalie said. But how sweet was it of Reed to bring her here? So sweet. They'd only been together for about five minutes, but he'd already made her feel so much better.

▲ ▲ ▲

Brynn thought doing a private practice session with Vern would make her feel better. More confident. But she kept messing up. Probably because she was trying so hard to prove to Vern that he had nothing to worry about. And it was totally clear that Vern was getting more and more worried. And frustrated. And angry. And Brynn-hating.

"Can we stop and go back to the beginning of

the scene?" Brynn asked after she'd gotten the same line wrong four times in a row.

"Is that what you're going to do in a performance?" Vern asked, reminding Brynn of Ms. Milligan. "Are you going to ask the audience if it's okay if we stop and go back to the beginning of the scene?"

"Of course not," Brynn answered.

"I wish I was as sure of that as you seem to be," Vern said. His eyes were definitely looking gray right now. He was in all-out serious mode. "Today is Wednesday, Brynn. We're going to be doing this scene for real on Saturday. This Saturday."

"I know that," Brynn said. She felt like throwing her head back and howling the words, but that definitely wouldn't reassure Vern. "And I'm going to be running lines every spare second I have. Rosemary's working with me tonight. And when no one is around to work with me, I'm going to use a tape recorder to check myself."

Vern nodded. "Okay, let's go back to the beginning of the scene. But no stopping this time." He cleared his throat and began. "There be some sports are painful, and their labour—"

He was interrupted by the opening song from *Hairspray* blasting out of Brynn's cell phone.

"Sorry, sorry, sorry," Brynn muttered as she dug through her backpack for the phone. She saw the name Jordan on the screen.

"You're not going to answer that, are you?" Vern demanded.

Brynn hesitated. "It will just take one second,

I swear," she answered. She couldn't pretend Jordan wasn't on the phone. That just wasn't right.

"Hi, Jordan. I can't talk right now," she said breathlessly.

"Why not?" he asked.

"I'm at Vern's. We're getting in a little extra rehearsal," she explained.

"Extra rehearsal? Come on, Brynn. You're at rehearsal practically all the time. I thought we could ride our bikes to the park."

Vern stared at her so hard it felt like her skin was being lasered off. "I can't, okay? Vern's waiting for me."

"Well, we don't want Vern to have to wait." The next sound Brynn heard was a click. Jordan had hung up on her!

▲ ▲ ▲

Tori checked her cell—for the seventh time that day. No little message icon on the screen. Where was Nat? What was her deal?

On the way home from the pier yesterday, she and Natalie had decided to get together if Nat's dad had plans. And he did. Anyone with a TV set knew that. There'd been about a million commercials for Oprah's *Live in LA* show, and every commercial showed Tad Maxwell. Oh, and did Tori mention the *live* part?

Maybe Natalie had sent her an e-mail. Although everyone knew that if you had something important to say, you called or texted. Tori headed into her bedroom and logged on to her e-mail account. An e-mail from Betsey Johnson—the store was having a sale. An e-mail from Bliss—sale. And one from Fornarina—big sale.

Tori wouldn't mind checking out the goods at any of the places. She could always use some more lemon butter from Bliss or another pair of shoes from Fornarina. But she didn't want to go by herself. Shopping was meant to be a social activity.

It's not as if Natalie was her only friend. That would be pretty pathetic. Nat didn't even live in the same state. But Char was skiing. Eva was in Texas with her parents visiting relatives. And Zandra was in Paris.

So forget shopping. There were other ways to have fun. Other ways called Michael. Tori shot her boyfriend an IM.

<Tori90210>: Hey, boy. What're you doing right now?
<MichaelS>: Hey, girl. Going to play soccer.
<Tori90210>: Do something with me instead.
<MichaelS>: You said you were busy the rest of the week with Nat.
<Tori90210>: Nat who?
<MichaelS>: Gotta go. Late.
<Tori90210>: Maybe I'll come watch. Where are you playing?

Tori let out a growl of frustration as the message "MichaelS is no longer available" appeared on her computer screen.

Michael was right. She was supposed to be doing

something with Nat. But, again, where was Nat? What was her deal?

Tori logged on to the camp blog. Maybe somebody there knew something about the mysterious disappearing Natalie Goode.

Posted by: Tori
Subject: Where, oh where, is Natalie?

Hey, everybody—
Anybody know what's going on with Nat? We were supposed to get together if her dad had plans, and right this minute, he's on television. Live television. Which I would call having plans.

I've called and texted her, but I haven't heard back. So have I been ditched or what?

Answer me. I know you're out there.

Tori

Within two minutes, Tori had three responses. She clicked on the first one and started to read.

From: Alyssa
Subject: Nat

Haven't heard from her, Tori.

If you guys go to that new exhibit at LACMA, the one with the meat under glass, I want to hear everything. It sounds really original. Gross, but original.

Alyssa

From: Valerie
Subject: Missing person

That's weird, Tori. It doesn't sound like Natalie.
Maybe she was talking about Thursday and not today?
Probably some mix-up like that.
Val

From: Jenna
Subject: Natalie

Maybe she's playing a game of hide-and-seek and
forgot to tell you.
Jenna
Joke of the day: How do scientists know the world
won't come to an end? Because it's round.

Very funny, Jenna, Tori thought. She flopped
down onto her bed and clicked on the TV.

Wednesday afternoon television. Great. Tori
flipped through the channels. One thing she knew for
sure—she didn't want to watch Tad Maxwell's giant face
smiling away. It was just a giant, smiling reminder that
Natalie had bailed on her. Without a phone call, a text
message, or even an e-mail.

chapter SIX

Natalie and Reed walked out of Grauman's Chinese Theater onto the cement patio covered with movie star handprints. "It's really true that the studios dump the most stinky movies into theaters in February," Natalie commented.

Reed widened his eyes in mock astonishment. "You didn't like the part where the guy and the alien went skiing together? I found the moment when the alien saw snow for the first time just so moving."

Natalie laughed. "I found it just so cheesy. But I always love going to movies here. Here and the Cinerama Dome." She turned and looked back at the theater. It was so cool how it had been designed in the style of a pagoda, with a huge dragon carved on the front and stone lion-dogs guarding the entrance.

Reed turned and looked at the red building with the green roof. "I forget how awesome it is. I just buy a ticket and head in without paying any attention."

"Yeah, I'm like that about a lot of the

amazing New York City stuff. If you see something too often, it's like it becomes partly invisible," Natalie answered. She turned and moved out of the way so a tourist could get a shot of John Wayne's handprints—with his buddy's hands positioned next to the prints. Tourists loved putting their hands next to the stars' to compare sizes.

"There's Bingley, right on time." Natalie nodded to the town car pulling up across the street. "You sure you don't want a ride?"

Reed shook his head. "We're pretty much on top of a subway," he answered. "So dinner at Baja Fresh on Friday night, right? The one on Sunset and Vine."

"Right," Natalie agreed. "I have to see the Elvis you say is always performing on the sidewalk."

"Kevin, the street Elvis," Reed corrected. "You can't forget the Kevin part. He's not so great at the fast stuff, like 'Jailhouse Rock.' But he does a killer 'Love Me Tender.'"

"I can't wait. I'll see you there at seven," Natalie told him. Then she headed for the car.

Bingley jumped out and opened the door for her. "Have fun?" he asked.

"I had the best time," she said as she climbed into the backseat.

"You might want to check your phone. It's been ringing a lot," Bingley said once he was behind the wheel.

"Oh, I did leave it here!" Natalie exclaimed. "I thought maybe I lost it. I had to use Reed's phone to tell you when to pick me up." She snatched the phone off the seat beside her. Wow. Three voicemail messages and eight text messages. Natalie listened to the voice-mail messages first.

"Hey, Nat Brat. It's Tors. Call me back."

Natalie clicked to the next message. It was from Tori, too. "Me again. I'm showered, dressed, blow-dried, and ready to go. Call me."

Oh, no. Oh, no, oh, no. Natalie had completely forgotten she'd told Tori they'd get together if her dad had plans. Dreading the rant she was going to hear, she moved on to the next message.

"Hey, it's Brynn. I need a little boyfriend advice. I might need to break up with Jordan, and I know you just did that with Logan. Call me. Or we can talk online. But call Tori first. She posted on the blog, and she seems kind of stressed that she hasn't heard from you."

Tori posted on the blog? She must be even more upset than Natalie thought she'd be. *Yikes.* She moved on to her text messages. She suspected some of them were going to be from Tori, too.

So what's the plan for today? Shopping, shopping, or shopping? I'm up for anything. But did I mention shopping? Tori

Hey, Nat. Tori posted on the blog. She's looking for you. She thinks you were supposed to be getting together with her. There's some communication confusion going on. Val

Could you take some pics of the Columbia Record

Building and zap them to me? I need them for an art class project. Zoom really close on the top, where it looks like a needle on a stack of records. (Those weird vinyl things.) Oh, and Tori's looking for you. Alyssa

Did you ditch Tori? If you did I wouldn't blame you. Just kidding. You know I'm nice now. Call her. She's trying to find you. Chelsea

N. WHERE. ARE. YOU? T.

Natalie didn't bother to read the rest of the messages. Clearly, she needed to call Tori RIGHT NOW!

She found Tori's name in her list of contacts and hit Send. *Please be there. Please pick up*, she thought as Tori's phone began to ring.

"Where are you?" Tori asked when she answered. She didn't bother giving Natalie a hello. "I thought we were supposed to get together if your father was busy. And I saw him on Oprah's show. Her *live* show."

"Tori, I'm so sorry!" Natalie burst out.

For one minute, Natalie thought about lying. She could tell Tori she'd spent the day hanging out in the green room at the TV studio while her dad did his interview. Then Tori couldn't be mad at her.

But she couldn't do that to Tori. It was bad enough that Natalie had forgotten their plans. Lying to her friend would just make the badness so much badder.

"I'm so sorry," Natalie said again. "I thought my

dad was going to be able to spend all day with me. Then I got up and saw his whole entourage having breakfast with him. It was so clear he wasn't going to have any time to spend with me—"

"Which is why you should have picked up the phone and called," Tori interrupted.

"I'm so sorry," Natalie said for the third time. "It's just that I'd read a text message from Reed right before I found out my father was going to be gone all day. Reed was kind of in my head when it happened, so I called him up and we decided to get together right then."

"So you just forgot all about me," Tori said, her voice sharp.

"Yeah," Natalie admitted. What else could she say? "I so suck," she added.

"You do," Tori agreed. "But I guess you were feeling kind of bad this morning when you found out your dad had all those plans."

"I was pretty miserable," Natalie answered. "And Reed, he kept me busy all day. You know the first place we went? My dad's star on the Walk of Fame. Reed said it was so I could spend some of the day with my father. How sweet was that?"

"Pretty sweet," Tori admitted. "Michael called me—"

"Pretty incredibly sweet," Natalie interrupted. Reed had been so much fun today. He'd almost made her forget that she hadn't spent any time with her father since she'd arrived in LA.

And he'd totally made her forget about her plans with Tori. And now just thinking about him had almost made her forget she was on the phone with her friend. *Yikes*.

"Do you want to hit the beach tomorrow, Tor?" Natalie asked. "I'm thinkin' Malibu."

"I could use a little Bu time," Tori said. "How about noon? Surfrider Beach?"

"I'm there. I'll bring lunch. You just bring you," Natalie answered. "I so owe you after today."

"Yeah, you do," Tori said. But she laughed, so Natalie knew she'd been forgiven.

Brynn created a private chat room, then waited. About thirty seconds later, Grace popped in, followed a few seconds later by Natalie.

<Grrrace>: Hey, B. I love how you decorated the room. ;)
<BrynnWins>: Nothing you say can make me laugh today.
<NatalieNYC>: maybe we should get jenna in here.
<BrynnWins>: No. I need serious help. Jenna isn't that good with serious. It's the Nat-Grace combo I need.
<Grrrace>: Tell us.
<BrynnWins>: I've been messing up incredibly at rehearsal. My lines just won't stay in my head.
<Grrrace>: Have you tried reciting your lines in bed, right before you fall asleep? That helps me.
<NatalieNYC>: i should ask my dad for advice . . . i'm not such the drama girl.
<BrynnWins>: It's not really the lines that are the problem.
<Grrrace>: But wait. You just said . . .

\<BrynnWins\>: I know, I know. And I am completely disgracing myself at rehearsal. I'm going to destroy the whole play if I don't get it together. What I need to do is spend every second practicing.

\<NatalieNYC\>: so why are you talking to us? go forth and shakespeare!

\<BrynnWins\>: The thing is, Jordan wants to hang out with me. It's vacation, and he has all this stuff he wants us to do together.

\<NatalieNYC\>: ah.

\<Grrrace\>: Oh. Well, Nat's more the boy expert than I am, but can't you just explain the sitch to him?

\<BrynnWins\>: I tried. And he hung up on me. I don't know what to do, you guys. The play opens this weekend, and it's such a big chance for me. Forget big. Huge, enormous, giganto! The *Globe* is going to review the show and everything. But Jordan's my boyfriend. And I can't totally ignore him, right? Grace, you're my drama girl. And, Nat, you know guys. What am I supposed to do?

\<Grrrace\>: As the drama girl, I have to say the play is the most important thing. You love theater, Brynn. We both know that. And doing Shakespeare, with a bunch of professional actors in the cast . . . that's huge squared. I'm jealous. And happy for you. And jealous. You've got to do whatever it takes to give your best performance.

\<BrynnWins\>: Except what it takes is completely ignoring Jordan.

\<NatalieNYC\>: maybe you should just be up front with him. tell him right now that until the play is over, you're going to have almost no free time.

<BrynnWins>: He'd probably just hang up on me again.

<Grrrace>: He should get how important the play is to you.

<NatalieNYC>: yeah, but, i can see how no brynn time makes for an unhappy bf. if brynn really can't see jordan for months, it's almost like they live in different states. and i know how hard that is. it's why logan and i decided to end it. well, logan decided, but he was right. the bad/ good thing is, i just met this really cool boy out in la. yes, la, as in across the country from me most of the time! ack!!

<BrynnWins>: So you're saying if Jordan can't accept me being tied up with the play, we should break up?

<Grrrace>: That's what I think.

<NatalieNYC>: i wasn't saying that, exactly. but maybe . . .

<Grrrace>: Ooooh. Except, what about Priya?

<BrynnWins>: Wait. What? What about what about Priya?

<NatalieNYC>: she's jordan's best friend. you do something to jordan, it's like you do it to priya.

<BrynnWins>: I don't want to break up with Priya. I don't even really want to break up with Jordan. But now I think I have to. He just doesn't get why I can't hang out with him *and* be in the play. But I can't. There's no way.

<Grrrace>: Good luck!

<NatalieNYC>: let us know how it goes.

<BrynnWins>: With Jordan or Priya?

<Grrrace>: Both!

Brynn logged off the computer, then she let her

head fall back and stared up at the ceiling. She was going to have to do it. She had no choice. She was going to have to break up with Jordan. She hoped she didn't end up minus a boyfriend and a regular friend. It would be horrible to mess up things with Priya, too.

SEVEN

Sunscreen—check. Beach towel—check. Magazines—check. Lip balm—check. Sunglasses—check. Beach umbrella—check. Aloe vera gel—check. Beach blanket—check. Evian water face spray—check. Hamper—check. Cooler—check. Cute beach hat—check.

Natalie had everything she needed for one fun-and-sun-filled day at the beach with Tori. She grabbed her beach bag, leaving the rest of the stuff for Bingley, and headed out the front door.

Her dad gave a quick double toot on the horn as he pulled his vintage Corvette Stingray convertible into the circular drive.

"Dad! What are you doing here?" Natalie exclaimed. "I thought you had back-to-back-to-back-to-back press conferences today."

He pulled to a stop in front of her. "I did. I do," he answered. "But while I was driving from the first one to the second one, it hit me." Her father grinned at her.

"What hit you?" she asked.

"That my favorite—and, okay, yes, only—daughter is in town, and I haven't spent any time with her." He leaned over and opened the Stingray's passenger door. "Get in. I'm taking you to lunch. I found a great new sushi place. And I know sushi is your favorite." His brow furrowed. "It's still your fave, right?"

"Right," Natalie said. She jumped in the car, leaving all her beach supplies behind. She knew she should tell her dad she had plans with Tori. But he might think she shouldn't cancel with a friend on such short notice. Which was true. She shouldn't.

She was going to, though. Tori would just have to understand. This might be the only time during her whole trip that Natalie could get some one-on-one time with her dad.

▲ ▲ ▲

Beach umbrella—Natalie's bringing. Sunscreen—check. Beach towel—check. Lip balm—check. Sunglasses—check. Aloe vera gel—check. Magazines—check. Evian water face spray—check. Cute beach hat—check. Beach blanket—Natalie's bringing. Hamper—Natalie's bringing. Cooler—Natalie's bringing.

Tori grabbed her beach bag. "Mom, come on!" she called. Her mother was going to drop her at Surfrider Beach, then hang poolside at her friend Jenny's place until Tori was ready to come home.

"Almost ready," her mother answered from the bathroom.

"Which means we'll be leaving in an hour," Tori muttered. Her cell phone rang. She dug it out of her bag and glanced at the screen. Michael. "Hi, boy," she said when she answered.

"Hey, girl. Whatcha doing?" he asked.

"I'm about to head to Malibu. If I can pry my mother away from the mirror." She shot an annoyed glance down the hall at the closed bathroom door.

"I could be up for Malibu," Michael hinted.

"Uh-uh. It's girl day. Natalie and I are going," Tori explained.

"How about if I ask Reed? He and Nat got along, right?" Michael said.

"Right. They got along so well that I barely saw Natalie when we were all at the pier," Tori explained.

Michael didn't say anything. Tori could picture the look on his face—all pouty. Michael insisted that boys didn't pout. But they so did. At least he did.

"She's only going to be here for a week—half a week now," Tori continued, trying to make him understand. "I'm not going to have many other chances to get together with her."

"What am I supposed to do today?" Michael asked. Tori almost laughed. He sounded soooo pouty!

"Poor boy. Like I'm your only friend," Tori said.

"You're my only girlfriend. At least you are unless you keep ditching me," Michael told her.

"I'm not ditching you. I told you before Natalie even got here that I wanted to hang with her as much as I could this week," Tori reminded him. She glanced at her watch. If she and her mother didn't leave in, well, two minutes ago, Tori was going to be late. "Gotta go," she told Michael. "I'll call you tonight."

"Bye," he said, and hung up.

He was not happy. Tori got that. But he'd live.

She looked at her watch again. "Mom, now please! I don't want Nat to be sitting on the beach by herself, waiting for me to show!"

▲ ▲ ▲

tors, can't meet you. dad free—for once! i'll call you later!

Natalie hit Send. No signal. Again! And she'd already tried to zap the message out eleven times. Plus she'd tried to call four times.

Tori is going to kill me, Natalie thought. She stared at the mountains rising up to the north, willing them to crumble into dust so she could get some cell phone service.

"We've covered school. What else is going on in your life?" her dad asked, pulling her away from her thoughts. Mostly. There was still a little part of her brain chanting, *Tori is going to kill me, Tori is going to kill me, Tori is going to kill me.*

Maybe she'd feel better if she just blurted out how bad and guilty she was feeling. But then maybe her dad would want to take her to meet Tori, and Natalie so, *so* didn't want to give up her time with him.

"Um, well you know I had a boyfriend," Natalie began.

"Logan," her father said.

"Right. Well, we kinda broke up," Natalie told him. *How mad is Tori right now?* she couldn't stop herself from wondering.

"Kinda?" Her father maneuvered around a curve.

"No, we did. It was too hard with us living so far apart. Maybe if we lived in the same city, we'd still be together. Probably. I mean, Logan's great," Natalie explained.

"You sound pretty okay with it," her dad observed. He was good at that—knowing how people were feeling. Natalie thought it was probably an actor thing. Actors had to understand emotions.

"Right before I came out, I was feeling bad. Lonely. I had the Logan Lonelies," Natalie admitted. *Is Tori going to be able to forgive me?*

"But spending so much time with your old dad took your mind off all that, am I right?" her father joked.

"Actually, not spending time with you helped a little," Natalie teased back.

"Ouch." Her dad slapped one hand to his chest.

"One day when I wasn't with you, Tori and I went to the Santa Monica Pier with her boyfriend and this other guy, Reed," Natalie explained. Now she really wished she'd spent more time with Tori that day. It was great hanging with Reed, but she and Tori had hardly talked.

She and her dad had hardly talked this trip, either. And now that she was with him, actually talking, she was thinking about how little she'd talked to Tori. *Arrgh!*

Her father laughed as he pulled into the parking lot of the tiny sushi place. "That was fast. How many days between old boy and new boy?"

"He's not my new boy," Natalie protested. "And maybe about eighteen days." She climbed out of the car and followed her dad around to the back of the restaurant. She tried to resend her text message to Tori as she walked. No signal.

She's going to kill me, Natalie thought. *Tori is totally going to kill me.*

"We have to eat out here," her father said. "The patio is the best thing about this place. Well, other than the food."

"It's great." Natalie looked around the patio—it was almost as big as the restaurant itself—trying to take in everything at once. The fountains, the flowers, the mosaic table tops. "I love how those morning glories wrap around the trunks of the palm trees." *Enjoy this place. Enjoy this lunch with your dad,* she ordered herself. *Deal with the Tori fallout later.*

Her dad took off his sunglasses and gave the nearest waitress what Natalie called The Smile. He used it at least once in every movie.

"Sit anywhere," the waitress said. She looked ready to kick people out of their seats if Tad Maxwell wanted her to.

"Here?" Natalie's dad asked Natalie, gesturing to the nearest table.

Natalie nodded. "I'm just going to run inside for a minute." She hurried inside the restaurant. "Do you have a pay phone?" she asked the bartender.

"What's a pay phone?" the guy asked. He looked kind of like Bingley. A lot of SoCali guys looked kind of like Bingley.

"One of those machines that you can put metal discs in and then talk to somebody who's not even in the same room with you," Natalie answered. With guys like him, guys who thought they were funny, it was usually better—or at least faster—just to play along.

"Sorry. This isn't a ye olde antique shop-pe," the bartender told her. He laughed. Guys like him, severely corny guys, always cracked themselves up. "But we've got one of these." He pulled a phone out from behind the bar and set it in front of Natalie. She reached for the receiver. The bartender grabbed her hand to stop her. "Local?"

"Local," Natalie promised, managing not to grit her teeth. As soon as the bartender released her hand, she punched in Tori's cell phone number. The cell rang and rang . . . and rang.

The mountains must be messing up her reception, too.

Slowly, Natalie hung up. There was nothing else she could do.

"Thanks," she told the bartender.

"I hope you live," he said solemnly.

"Me too," Natalie said as she headed back out to the patio.

"I ordered you a blackberry iced tea," her dad told her.

Natalie took a long, long drink. She really had done everything she could to get in touch with Tori. Now she had to forget about her friend and have a fun lunch with her father. It was practically the first time they'd had a meal together her whole visit.

"So tell me more about this new boy, Reed," her dad urged.

"Reed, he's—"

"Stop," her father interrupted. "First tell me what's wrong."

He was good.

And Natalie couldn't hold all the bad feelings inside one second longer. She took a deep breath and let it spew. "It's just that I was supposed to get together with Tori yesterday, and I forgot. I just . . . forgot. So we made plans to get together today. But then you—"

"Decided to take you to lunch with no advance notice," her dad filled in. "I didn't even ask you if you had plans."

"I wanted to go with you. I did. But now Tori's going to think I forgot all about her. I tried to text her and call her, but the texts didn't go through and then I got her voicemail," Natalie went on. "She's probably sitting on Surfrider Beach right now, planning the most painful way to massacre me."

"Nat, Surfrider Beach is only about ten minutes from here. Let's go," her father said.

"Seriously?" Natalie asked, a wave of relief breaking over her.

"Of course, seriously," he answered. "I'll take you both out to lunch."

She was going to get to spend time with Tori *and* her dad. The perfect solution.

Her father stood up. "We'll be back in twenty," he called to the waitress. "And we'll need another place setting." He gave The Smile.

"You got it," the waitress answered.

"She might not even be there," Natalie said. "I was supposed to meet her fifteen minutes ago."

Natalie's father gave Natalie The Smile. "She'll still be there."

chapter

EIGHT

Tori strode through the front door and went directly to her room. No passing Go. No collecting two hundred dollars. She logged right on to her computer. She had a lot to say, and she absolutely could not wait to say it. She just cracked her knuckles, then began to type.

Posted by: Tori
Subject: Natalie is dead to me

REMEMBER THE OTHER DAY WHEN I WAS LOOKING FOR NATALIE? WELL, SHE WAS OUT WITH A BOY. A BOY *I* FOUND FOR HER, THANK YOU VERY MUCH. SHE DIDN'T EVEN REMEMBER WE WERE SUPPOSED TO MEET UP.

BUT I FORGAVE HER. I DID. I MADE PLANS WITH HER AGAIN. WE WERE SUPPOSED TO GO TO THE BEACH TOGETHER. SO I SAT THERE WAITING AND SHE NEVER SHOWED UP. SHE IS THE WORST PERSON EVER! SELFISH AND INCONSIDERATE AND EVERYTHING BAD!!

AND YES, I KNOW I'M SHOUTING. I NEED TO SHOUT. AAAAAAGH!!!

TORRRRRIIIIEEE

"Aaaaaagh!" Tori screamed. She jumped up from the computer, paced back and forth across her bedroom four times, clicked on the TV, flipped through all the channels, clicked off the TV, turned on the radio, trolled through all the stations, turned it off, put her iPod on, listened to half of five songs, turned it off, and then sat down to check the blog. She wanted to read all about how everyone now hated Natalie as much as she did.

Posted by: Grace
Subject: Don't scream

Don't scream at me, Tori. I know you don't want to hear this right now, but I think you should wait and see what Natalie has to say about not showing up. She could have a good explanation. Even though she didn't the other time. (Unless the boy she was hanging with was shirtless. Tee hee.)

Natalie is really a good friend. She completely talked Brynn through a problem yesterday. Just give her a chance, okay?

Grace

Posted by: Priya
Subject: What's Brynn's problem?

Jordan didn't say anything to me about any prob. And those two tell each other everything. It's kind of nauseating!

Priya

Posted by: Valerie
Subject: Missing Natalie

Um, just go read my other "Missing Natalie" message. I know that it turned out that she did sort of ditch you last time. But it really isn't like Nat to forget about her friends. Maybe she a) got sunstroke which led to amnesia, b) never learned why one hand on the watch is big and one is little, c) there has to be a c. I'll write again when I think of one.
Val

Posted by: Alyssa
Subject: Nat

Natalie is a great friend. Listen to Grace's advice, okay? Just wait and see what Natalie says about why she didn't show. It's weird that this happened twice.

Nat, is something wrong? Is something going on we should know about?

Even Alyssa thinks there's something wrong with Nat, Tori thought. *And Alyssa's her best friend at camp.*

Tori exited the blog. She didn't need to wait around and see how Natalie answered Alyssa's question. Tori already new exactly what was wrong with Natalie. She was a horrible, selfish, inconsiderate, bad, bad person.

Brynn sat on the edge of the fountain in the middle of the mall. Where was Jordan? They were supposed to meet here—she checked her watch—four minutes ago. Four! And she didn't have any minutes to spare. She should be going over her lines right now. The first performance of the play was in two days. Two!

Tonight was a dress rehearsal. Ms. Milligan said they had to go on no matter what happened—just like it was a performance. Brynn thought she had her part down. She'd been working on it almost nonstop. But she didn't want to make a single mistake. Why hadn't she brought a copy of the script with her to the mall? And where was Jordan?

In a way, Brynn wished he'd pull a no-show, the way Nat kept doing to Tori. That way, she could just get really mad at him and break up. Instead of actually having The Talk and telling him she couldn't be his girlfriend—at least not the way he wanted her to—and be in the play at the same time.

A few droplets of water hit Brynn on the back of the neck, startling her away from her thoughts. She looked over her shoulder and saw Jordan and Priya grinning at her.

"He did it." Priya pointed to Jordan.

"She did it," Jordan said at the same time, pointing to Priya.

Oh, no, Brynn thought. *What is Priya doing here?* There was no way she could have The Talk with Jordan if Priya was around.

She flashed on what Grace had said in the chat room. About Priya being mad at Brynn if Brynn broke things off with Jordan. Brynn looked over at Priya. Was that true?

"Hey, you guys," Brynn said.

"Hope you don't mind that I came with Jordan. We're going to a Bar Mitzvah party for a kid in our class. We wanted to go in on a present together," Priya told her.

"Sure. Great," Brynn answered. Priya was her friend. It's not like Brynn could tell her to get lost. That would definitely make Priya mad!

"Sorry about the other day. When I, you know . . ." Jordan said.

"When he hung up on you," Priya explained.

Brynn and Jordan hadn't seen each other face-to-face since the hang-up. They hadn't talked on the phone, either. They'd made arrangements to meet at the mall via e-mail.

"I know it bothers you how much time I'm spending on the play," Brynn answered. That's all she thought she could say without starting The Talk.

"Vacation is supposed to be when you can hang with your friends," Priya commented, making it clear whose side she was on. As if there was ever any doubt she'd side with Jordan.

But that didn't necessarily mean she'd be angry if Brynn broke up with Jordan. Just that she'd think Brynn was wrong and Jordan was right. But that didn't mean Priya wouldn't want to be Brynn's friend anymore. Did it?

"So what kind of present do you want to get?" Brynn asked. She definitely needed a subject change.

"Kyle is into science stuff," Jordan answered.

"So we should hit the Discovery Store," Priya said.

"It's upstairs, I think," Brynn told them.

Jordan and Priya looked at each other and laughed. "It's about fifteen feet from where you're sitting," Jordan told her.

"It's okay, Brynn. We know you're not a science kind of person," Priya said as she led the way into the store.

"Just like we're not drama kind of people," Jordan added.

Wow, the two of them talk like they're identical in every way, Brynn thought.

"Remember when we were trying to come up with smart stuff for you to say to Brynn when you two went to that play together in D.C.?" Priya asked Jordan. They laughed together again.

"I remember that what you two came up with was pretty silly," Brynn said.

"But you still ended up with Jordan," Priya reminded her.

Brynn nodded, thinking about how much fun she and Jordan had had together since that day in D.C. And now she was breaking up with him. At least she was if she ever had the chance to talk to him alone.

Don't think about it now, Brynn told herself. *It's pointless.* She picked up a box from the closest display. "Hey, they have an electronic *Deal or No Deal*," she announced.

"That's so not Kyle," Priya said.

Jordan picked up a game. "How about this? Brainiac in a Box?"

"That so *is* Kyle," Priya said. "How much?"

"Less than we thought we'd have to spend," Jordan answered. "Want to get it?"

"Let's look around a little more," Priya told him. "Is that guy Martin going to be at the party? Because if he is, I'm not going."

"You don't even know him," Jordan protested.

"I don't need to know him," Priya shot back. "I know what he did to you that time at the soccer game. That's all I need to know."

"It wasn't that big a deal. And it was almost a year ago," Jordan reminded her.

"Who cares? It was still a rotten thing to do to you," Priya said, her voice hard.

Yikes, Brynn thought. *I really might lose a friend and a boyfriend when I break up with Jordan.*

Natalie shoved the laptop off her stomach and onto the bed beside her. She felt like throwing it out the window and into the swimming pool.

The things Tori had written about her . . . Just reading them had made Nat feel battered and bruised.

It was so unfair. She'd tried to text Tori. And Natalie and her dad had gone to Surfrider Beach looking for her. They'd gotten to the beach twenty minutes late. Just twenty minutes! Tori could have waited that long. She didn't know that Natalie had tried to cancel. None of Natalie's voicemails or texts had gotten through.

She could have waited until she'd talked to Nat before she posted all that trash on the camp blog, too.

Not just could have. *Should* have.

Now everyone from camp was taking about Natalie and what could be wrong with her. At the very least, Tori should have put her tirade in a private e-mail.

Natalie sat up on the bed and pulled the laptop in front of her. The camp blog still filled the screen. Tori's screaming post was near the top.

Was she really supposed to apologize to Tori in front of everyone—after Tori had called Natalie all those names? Nat hesitated, her fingers poised over the laptop keys.

Natalie had definitely done something she should apologize for. But now so had Tori. Did the two needed apologies basically cancel each other out? Nat wasn't sure.

All she knew was that she wasn't ready to post to the blog. Not yet, anyway. Instead she began to compose an e-mail to her best Camp Lakeview friend.

To: Alyssa11
From: NatalieNYC
Subject: nothing's wrong

hey, lyss

i know you think something might be wrong, since i went no-show on tori—twice. but nothing's wrong.

well, actually, the first time i was supposed to meet up with tor there was maybe a little something wrong. i was supposed to do something with my dad that day (tori and i had agreed to get together if my dad couldn't hang with me) and when my dad canceled on me, i was pretty upset. and this guy reed that tori had introduced me to had left me a message. i called him, and he cheered me up and we decided to meet up. and i forgot about tori. i just forgot. maybe if i hadn't been so mad and sad over the dad sitch i would have remembered. i don't know.

today my dad finally had time to take me to lunch. it was almost the first time we'd been able to see each other since i arrived. there was no way i could say no to him. and i didn't want to.

i kept trying to call and text tori, but there was no signal. the santa monica mountains should be burned to the ground. except that i don't think you can burn dirt. my father realized i was upset, and when i told him why, we went to the beach where i was supposed to meet tori. she wasn't there. even though i was only a few minutes late. i'm really sorry that i wasn't there on time. at least i was sorry until i read that nasty post tori wrote about me on the blog. now i'm almost as mad at her as she is at me.

help, alyssa. what am i supposed to do here?!
confused in california,
nat

A reply from Alyssa popped into Natalie's inbox almost immediately. That's the kind of friend Alyssa was.

To: NatalieNYC
From: Alyssa11
Subject: Confused in California

Dear Confused,

I'm no Dear Abby or anything, but I know what you need to do. Apologize.

I know, I know. Tori wrote really mean things about you. And if she asked me what to do, I'd tell her to apologize to you, too. But you sort of started it, even though you tried to get in touch with her and even find her on the beach. Just call her and tell her what you told me.

And, Nat—do it fast. It's only going to get worse between the two of you if you don't. You were both born under stubborn signs!

Love and luck,

Alyssa

Natalie let herself flop back onto her pillows. Alyssa was right. Natalie needed to apologize. And she would. She just needed a few minutes—or a few hours—to forget some of what Tori had written about her.

Then Natalie would definitely say she was sorry. It wouldn't be easy, but she'd do it.

chapter
NINE

To: imnotmichaelJORDAN
From: BrynnWins
Subject: You and me

Hi, Jordan,

I wish we'd had some time by ourselves at the mall yesterday. Not that I wasn't happy to see Priya. Priya's the best. But there was something I wanted to talk to you about in person. But I can't wait until the next time we're together. Since as you totally know, we aren't together that much lately.

Ack! I'm so bad at this. This is so hard to say. Even to type say. I know you don't like how busy I've been with the play. And I have to tell you that I'm not going to be able to change that. *The Tempest* opens tomorrow—as you also totally know, since I talk about the play way too much! It probably seems like I'll have a ton more free time after that. But I won't. We have a performance almost every night, which means when I'm not onstage, I'll be doing homework. (If I don't, I'll be dead. Murdered by my parents.)

So for the next few months, I won't be able to see you much at all. Maybe once or twice, but that's it. It will be like you hardly have a girlfriend. So I was thinking, maybe it would be better if we just agreed not to be boyfriend and girlfriend until after the play, ya know?

I hope you understand.

Brynn

Brynn hit Send without reading over the e-mail. It was hard enough to write it.

She glanced at the hula girl clock on her desk. She had to leave for rehearsal in less than an hour. How was she supposed to transform herself into Miranda when all she could think about was Jordan and how he was going to feel when he read her message?

Shower, she decided. *You need to take a shower.* Brynn had actually taken a shower when she first got up this morning, about three hours ago. But one of her acting books said you should take a shower before a performance and imagine all your personal junk—worries, fears, angry thoughts, whatever—running down the drain with the water. That way there's nothing to block the character you're playing.

Brynn hurried to the bathroom, tossed off her clothes, and jumped into the shower. She turned on the spray as hot as she could stand it. She loved it when steam filled the little room, even though her dad was always telling her that someday firemen were going to break down the door, thinking the house was on fire.

She studied the bottles of bath gel in the plastic

rack that was stuck to the shower wall with little suction cups, and then reached for the Mandarin orange. Jordan loved the smell of oranges.

Jordan. Had he read her e-mail yet? Was he upset? Mad? Had he told Priya? Had—

Stop! Brynn ordered herself. The whole point of the shower was to get rid of all her worries about Jordan and Priya and everything else. She needed to be ready to transform herself into Miranda. She'd been working so hard, squeezing in extra rehearsals with Vern, going over her script until her eyes felt hot and heavy, skipping all her favorite TV shows to recite her lines in front of the mirror. She couldn't let anything stop her from delivering the awesome performance she knew was in her.

So definitely no Mandarin orange. Brynn stuck the bottle back into the rack and grabbed the deep maroon bottle of fig and flower scented gel. Figs and flowers. Miranda's island probably had figs and flowers growing on it.

She closed her eyes and she poured some of the gel into her hands. She sucked in a deep lungful of the lush perfume—and steam—and imagined that she was the girl who had never seen another human but her father. Until Ferdinand, with his green eyes and—

No. Vern was playing Ferdinand, and Vern's eyes were smoky blue-gray. Jordan's eyes were green.

Brynn sighed. Washing personal stuff down the drain was a lot harder than the acting book had made it sound.

She got out of the shower twenty minutes later. Her fingers and toes were wrinkly, but she felt ready to have a triumphant dress rehearsal. She was going to *become* Miranda.

Brynn grabbed a towel and dried off as fast as she could. Being late definitely wasn't part of her plan to be triumphant. She whipped on her clothes, then bounded out into the hallway. "Dad, we need to leave for the theater!" she called.

"Give me five," he called back.

"Okay," she answered. They had five to spare. Barely.

She headed for the kitchen to get a granola bar for the road. But she paused as she started past her bedroom. Through the half-open door she could see her computer.

Had Jordan read her e-mail yet? Had he already answered her?

Don't check until you come home, Brynn told herself. *You just practically washed yourself down the drain so you wouldn't be thinking about Jordan during rehearsal.*

Her feet walked themselves over to her desk. Like they had a mind of their own. Her rear planted itself in the chair in front of the computer. Her fingers logged on to her e-mail account. Her eyes checked the messages.

There was one new one. From Priya.

Brynn's throat turned to a desert, dry and scratchy. She didn't want to read that e-mail. But she couldn't stop herself. She clicked it open.

To: BrynnWins
From: Priyadayada
Subject: What you did

I don't believe you, Brynn. Jordan is the best guy in the world—even if you don't think so. And you break up with him. In an e-mail!

He can't even answer you right now. That's how much you hurt him. So I'm answering for him. I'm glad you broke up with him. You just proved he deserves a lot better. Go be with one of your drama boys, like you want to.

Don't expect Jordan or me to be hanging with you at camp this summer.

Priya

▲ ▲ ▲

"Yes?" Michael said, pretending not to recognize Tori when he saw her standing on his porch.

She raised her eyebrows. She was so not in the mood.

"If you're selling something, we don't do door-to-door," he told her.

So *extremely* not in the mood. Tori pushed past Michael and headed to the den. She curled up in her favorite chair, the one with the built-in massager. "What did you rent?"

Michael held up a DVD case that had a bunch of snakes coiled around a bus on the front.

Tori rolled her eyes. "Movies go straight to video for a reason, you know," she told him.

"No one's forcing you to watch it," Michael shot

back. He shoved the disc into the DVD player.

"Sorry," Tori muttered. "It's Natalie I'm mad at, not you."

Michael let out a dramatic groan. "We've barely hung out since Natalie showed up. And now that we are, she's still wrecking things." He flopped down on the sofa and picked up the remote. "And anyway, I thought she left you a message apologizing."

"She did. Two," Tori admitted. "I deleted them. I can't even stand to hear her voice right now."

A sliver of guilt poked at her. She ignored it. She had nothing to feel guilty about. An apology—or two—didn't make everything okay.

"Whatever," Michael said. "You're still letting her stop us from having fun. And it's not like she isn't going to be out having a good time tonight."

"What?" Tori demanded.

"Nothing," Michael answered quickly. "Let's just watch the movie. You thought the first one was funny. That's why I got this one." He clicked on the TV.

"Wait. Don't start it. I want to know exactly what you meant about Natalie having a good time tonight." Tori stared at Michael, willing him to talk.

"Fine. But you're not going to like it," Michael finally said. "Reed told me he and Nat are going out to dinner tonight."

"Oh, that's perfect." Tori snatched her purse off the floor and yanked out her cell phone. She hit Natalie's speed dial number. She promised herself she was erasing Natalie from her phone as soon as she hung up. This was the last time she wanted to talk to her so-called friend.

"Hello," Natalie said.

"I got your messages and I don't care that you're sorry. Or at least that you say you are," Tori said in a rush, anger bringing a flush to her cheeks and the back of her neck.

"But, Tori, I tried to get in touch with you and tell you what was going on. It's not my fault I couldn't get a signal," Natalie protested.

"There were no signal problems the day you were hanging out with Reed," Tori snapped. "You hardly even know him and you're spending more time with him than me. We're supposed to be friends."

"I thought we were past that," Natalie said. "I apologized, you accepted. You said you understood that I was upset about my dad canceling on me at the last minute. I shouldn't have forgotten we said we'd get together if my father was busy. But like I said, I was up-set." She said the last word slowly, like she was talking to a toddler.

"Are you going to be upset again tonight?" Tori asked.

"What are you talking about?" Natalie responded.

"I know you're going out with Reed tonight," Tori informed her. Michael slapped his hands over his face and shook his head.

"If you'd called me back after either of the mes-sages I left you, I was going to see if you wanted to come. I really did want to spend a lot of time with you while I was here," Natalie said.

"Yeah, it really shows," Tori replied.

"Look, Tori, I'm trying to be nice here," Natalie said. "Even though you went on the blog and completely trashed me in front of everybody."

"You deserved it!" Tori cried.

"No I didn't. You didn't even call me. You went behind my back and started crying to all our friends," Natalie answered, her voice getting higher and higher.

"All I did was tell the truth." Tori brushed her long blond hair away from her face with her free hand. "You are selfish and thoughtless and everything else I wrote."

"If you think that, you shouldn't care that I'm going out with Reed tonight," Natalie yelled. "You shouldn't ever want to see me again."

"I don't!" Tori shouted back.

"Then forget about going to the Academy Awards with me." Natalie hung up without giving Tori a chance to respond.

Tori snapped her phone shut. She should have been the one to hang up first. Natalie really was *so* selfish.

chapter

TEN

Flashes went off from a bunch of cameras as Natalie, Reed, and both their fathers walked past the white picket fence outside the Ivy, a restaurant where everyone who was anyone dined. Flashes were always going off outside the Ivy. A pack of paparazzi practically lived across the street, using their telephoto lenses to catch the stars.

Natalie spotted Jessica Biel *and* Will Ferrell as soon as she stepped inside. The host led them to a table right next to the fireplace.

"Primo table. Impressive," Reed whispered to Natalie.

Natalie nodded. She'd been in Hollywood often enough to know that the more powerful someone was in the film industry, the better the table they got at the Ivy and all the other celebrity hot spots.

"If we can get along as well as these two, we should definitely do the movie together," Reed's father said. He and Natalie's father were thinking of working on a project together—Reed's dad directing, Natalie's starring. When they'd heard Reed and Natalie were meeting up for dinner, they'd decided to crash and talk business. And they insisted on coming to the Ivy, where most of the important deals in Hollywood were made.

Natalie smiled at Mr. Garrett. "Please do it," she begged him. "You're supposed to be able to get an amazing performance out of any actor. Even an action star like my dad."

"Excuse me," her dad said. "An action star who has been nominated for an Oscar."

"What he's saying is he wants big, big bucks," Mr. Garrett explained to Reed and Natalie.

Their waiter approached, looking spiffy in the Ivy uniform, a pink shirt with roses scattered across it. "The usual?" he asked Mr. Garrett.

Mr. Garrett nodded. "I love the fried chicken here so much, I never get anything else."

"I'll give the rest of you time to look over the menu," the waiter said.

"All I care about is dessert," Reed commented. "They have the best desserts in the world here."

"We came here for Reed's last birthday," Mr. Garrett said. "He had dessert for every course. Appetizer, main, and, of course, dessert."

"The desserts here *are* awesome," Natalie told Reed as their fathers turned to talking about business. "But the best dessert in the world? No way. New York has the best dessert. Serendipity's frozen hot chocolate."

"Let me ask you this. Have you had the fudgie pecan brownie here?" Reed asked.

"No," Natalie admitted. "But I've had lots of the other desserts, and—"

"Until you've had the brownie, I'm not talking to you," Reed interrupted.

"Fine. But you've got to admit that New York has the best pizza," Natalie said.

"No contest. Famous Original Ray's," Reed agreed.

"Okay. I'm glad you said that. Now we can stay friends," Natalie told him.

As soon as the words were out of her mouth, she thought of Tori. Their phone call had gotten so nasty. They were never going to be able to be friends again. Natalie didn't even want to think about how it would be at camp this summer.

"Maybe we can be friends," Reed said. "But there are a few more things we have to discuss. Let's talk baseball teams."

Natalie laughed, and a little of the stress that had been knotting up her shoulders ever since she hung up on Tori slid away. Reed was so cool. "Hey, do you want to go to the Oscars with me?" she blurted out.

"Really?" Reed asked. "Even my dad couldn't score tix this year. He doesn't have anything nominated."

"Dad managed to get a pair for me and a friend. So are you coming with me or not?" Natalie teased.

"I'm coming. Are you kidding? Of course I'm coming," Reed answered. Then he frowned. "But, wait, I thought Michael told me you were taking Tori."

The word Tori was like a punch to Natalie's gut. "Um, Tori and I . . ." She really didn't want to go into the whole thing. She felt like she might start screaming—or crying—if she talked about it too much. "Tori and I, we thought it might be fun if I had an actual date. You know, a guy type person."

Reed might find out the truth from Michael—although guys didn't seem to talk about real stuff as much as girls did—but Natalie would deal with that if it happened.

"Well, I'm very happy to be your guy type person," Reed told her.

"Great!" Natalie exclaimed.

She'd have fun with Reed. She would. And it was Tori's own fault that Natalie was giving her ticket to someone else.

▲ ▲ ▲

Brynn watched as the storm started up onstage. It was so beautiful, beautiful and scary at the same time. The crashing waves were created by actors dressed in skintight blue and green unitards rolling and sliding and hurling themselves across the stage, waving long, long scarves.

The shipwreck was about to happen. Then there was a short scene with the men on the ship, then Brynn's first scene. She had about five minutes, so she tiptoed into the lobby of the theater and called Grace.

"I can only talk for a second," she burst out as soon as Grace answered. "I'm on the cell, and it's not free minutes yet. I need you to do me a huge favor. Will you check my e-mail for me? I sent Jordan a breakup e-mail and I have to know if he answered. My cell is so prehistoric, I can't use it to check my inbox."

"You broke up with him over e-mail?" Grace exclaimed.

"Never mind about that part. We can talk about that later. I just need to know if Jordan answered. Priya said he was too hurt," Brynn told her.

"So Priya was okay with the whole thing? She's not mad?" Grace asked.

"No, you were right. Priya is probably planning how she can get away with murdering me right now. She completely hates me," Brynn said. "But what I care about is Jordan. Just go into my e-mail account. My password is—"

"You're not supposed to give anyone your password," Grace interrupted.

"You're my best friend!" Brynn exclaimed. "I trust you. And if it'll make you feel better, I'll change the password tonight."

"Okay, tell me," Grace said.

"It's—don't laugh. It's stargirl, all one word," Brynn said. "So go on. If Jordan answered, call me back and read what he said. If he didn't answer, call me back and tell me. And hurry. I have to go onstage in, like, three minutes, and I can't wait until my scene is over to know what's going on."

"I'm on it." Grace hung up.

Brynn paced back and forth across the red carpet of the lobby. She was so not in Miranda's head right now. The shower thing had not worked at all. All her worries about Jordan and Priya felt like they were stuck to her with superglue.

"Come on, Grace. Come on," she muttered. Then she took a deep breath and started to count. "One Mississippi, two Mississippi, three Mississippi . . ." Her cell rang at twenty-three Mississippi.

"Talk fast," Brynn said instead of hello.

"Sorry. No e-mail from Jordan," Grace told her.

"Okay. Okay." Brynn felt tears sting her eyes and she blinked them away. "Well, that's . . . I wanted to know that. I'll talk to you later."

"Sorry," Grace said again. "Bye."

"Bye." Brynn closed her phone. She opened the door to the theater to see how far the first scene had gotten. Very far. She needed to get to her place backstage. Now.

Had she really hurt Jordan that badly? So badly he couldn't even communicate with her? Just thinking about it had tears stinging Brynn's eyes again.

Use the emotion, she told herself. Another acting book had advised that. It had said to use every emotion you felt in your regular life in your craft. In the scene Brynn was about to do, Miranda was supposed to be distraught and horrified over the shipwreck that had just happened.

Distraught and horrified. Brynn could do that. It would be way too easy.

Tori's cell gave a meow. If that was Natalie texting an apology, she could forget it. There was nothing she could say that would make Tori forgive her.

"You're missing the best part," Michael complained as Tori flipped open her phone. "The giant snake is about to eat half the boat."

"Michael, it's our third snake movie of the night. I think I've seen pretty much everything a snake of any size can do," Tori told him as she checked her message. It was from Chelsea.

Pix of Nat all over the Internet. Check out LAglitz. And check out the big smile on her face. Guess she's not too upset by your post on the blog, huh?

Tori snapped her cell closed and leaped to her feet.

"Hey, where are you going?" Michael called as she strode from the room.

She rushed to the closest computer—the one in the kitchen—and logged on. She typed "LAglitz" into Google, and in seconds she had the site open with Natalie's big, stupid grinning face staring at her.

"I didn't know the dads were going with Reed and Natalie," Michael said as he leaned over her shoulder to get a closer look at the picture. "Guess that's why they ended up at the Ivy."

The Ivy. Nice. Natalie was out at a swanky place, surrounded by celebs—and a very cute boy that *Tori* had introduced her to. That smile made it very clear she was having big fun.

It also made it clear that she didn't care at all about the fight she and Tori had had. Very nice.

ELEVEN

"So what do you think? Best hot dog—Pink's here or Gray's Papaya in New York?" Reed asked. He and Natalie stood on the sidewalk near Pink's hot dog stand, one of the most popular places in Hollywood. There was always a line at Pink's, no matter what time of day.

Natalie took another bite of her Guadalajara dog—relish, onions, and tomatoes topped with sour cream. She chewed slowly, trying to think about Reed's question. But what she ended up thinking about was Tori. Tori loved Pink's. And she and Natalie had planned to come have hot dogs together after the Academy Awards. They were going to swing by before the Governor's Ball. In their fancy clothes. In the limo. It would be just like when Hillary Swank went to Astro Burger with her Oscar.

"Well?" Reed prompted.

She couldn't tell him that she hadn't even tasted her hot dog. She'd been eating, but not tasting. "Tough call," she answered. She tossed the last bit of the dog into the trash. If she wasn't going to taste it, why eat it?

"That's sacrilegious," Reed said. "Nobody throws away a Pink's."

"Usually I'd be getting in line for a second. But my stomach is all knotted," Natalie admitted. "Maybe I'm just nervous about the Oscars. Nervous for my dad. He's never been nominated before."

"Mine's been nominated three times. Never won. I think he's kind of looking forward to watching the whole thing on the tube tonight. He hates dressing up," Reed replied.

"I love it. And speaking of dressing up . . ." She checked her watch. "I should go. I have a fitting in a little bit. Lulu's doing my dress. She won *Project Runway* last year. Do you watch it?" Natalie asked.

"Hello. I'm a guy type person, remember?" Reed asked.

"Oh, right," Natalie said, like she'd just realized it.

Tori would know who Lulu is, Natalie couldn't help herself from thinking.

"So, I guess I'll see you later," Reed told Natalie.

"Yep," she answered, forcing a smile. Then she gave him a quick hug and walked over to the town car. Bingley was leaning against it, finishing a chili cheese dog. "These things should be illegal," he said as he opened the door for Nat. "They are that good."

"Uh-huh," Natalie said. She hadn't even managed to get her whole hot dog down, and she was feeling nauseous. *This should be an amazing day*, she thought as they began the drive home. *Pink's with Reed.*

And now I'm about to meet Lulu, who is going to show me her new designs. Which I'll be wearing to the Academy Awards. Why does it feel like I've been to the dentist and am now about to take back-to-back tests in every subject? Even ones I've never heard of.

She let out a sigh. *Come on. Don't let Tori ruin everything,* she pep-talked herself. *You did everything you could. You apologized and explained, then apologized and explained some more. It's not your fault Tori is stubborn and unforgiving and horrible.*

"Looks like your dress shop has arrived," Bingley commented, pulling into the circular driveway. He nodded to two young guys pushing a wheeled clothing rack toward the house, followed by Lulu. She'd changed her hair since she was on the TV show. Now it was in a sleek bob, a pale lavender sleek bob.

Tori would love that, Natalie thought.

Why did she have to keep thinking about Tori?

"You have to be Natalie," Lulu called as Nat climbed out of the car.

"I have to be," Natalie agreed.

"We're going to have fun. I brought over all my newest stuff for us to play with. I just started a line I'm calling A-Tire. It's clothes that are made out of recycled tires and inner tubes. I got really into recycled material after we had that junkyard challenge on *Runway*."

Natalie opened the front door for the guys with the clothes rack. They wheeled it in to the large foyer. "Stop here," Lulu told them. "The rack's a pain to move around. Why don't we grab some stuff you like and then take them to your room? Does that work?"

"Sounds great," Natalie answered.

"Excellent." Lulu took off her huge sunglasses, then pulled a long, black dress off the rack. "This is one of the A-Tire ones. I found a way to get the rubber soft enough to ruffle. Feel."

Natalie reached out and fingered one of the shiny ruffles that cascaded from the neck of the dress all the way to the floor. It was really soft. "I love the train," she told Lulu.

"I used cloth to line it." Lulu flipped part of the train over, showing the funky pink-and-black plaid material underneath. "Just for a kicky little surprise detail." She handed Natalie the gown, then studied her for a moment. "I definitely want you to try on something from my Camouflage line."

Lulu selected a pair of pants in the pink-and-black plaid that she'd used as lining for the train of the first dress. Then she pulled out a short jacket of the same pink-and-black plaid. And gloves of pink-and-black plaid. And a hood of pink-and-black plaid.

"That is one heck of a lot of plaid," Natalie murmured.

Lulu grinned. "I know. I like to be excessive. It's going to look adorable on you, though. I promise." Lulu flipped through the rack. "What else? What else?"

Natalie watched her, still feeling sort of nauseous. She loved clothes. And she was about to try on outfits by her favorite designer. She should be in ecstasy. But she wasn't. She was in anti-ecstasy. It was no fun playing dress-up alone.

"What's wrong? You love clothes. There are clothes all around you. There's only one reason I agreed to come to Plaid & Stars," Michael told Tori. "I thought it was impossible for you to be unhappy here."

"I'm happy. And it's Polkadots & Moonbeams," Tori said as she fingered the big flowers embroidered on a sweater.

"You're happy," Michael repeated, sounding disgusted. "You're a liar is what you are."

Tori moved on to a selection of flapper dresses. All the vintage stuff at Polkadots had been cleaned and repaired. You didn't have to go digging through piles of smelly, holey things. Tori hated doing that.

She selected an emerald green dress and held it up in front of her, the dress's fringe swinging against her legs. It was cool. Retro and hip at the same time. It looked like the kind of thing Mandy Moore might wear. *It could have been my dress for the Oscars*, Tori thought. *If Nat and I were still friends.*

"That looks like it would fit you perfectly," the college-aged sales clerk said. "Do you want to try it on?"

Tori hung the dress back up. "No, thanks. I don't really have any place to wear it."

In a day and a half, Natalie would be gone. She'd be three thousand miles away, back in New York. Maybe then Tori would stop thinking about her all the time.

Maybe.

When am I going to stop thinking about Jordan all the time? Brynn asked herself. *When?*

Clearly not anytime soon, she thought as she walked over to her computer. Again. And checked her e-mail. Again. And there was no e-mail from Jordan. Again.

It had been a whole day since Brynn had sent him the breakup e-mail. What was he thinking? Was he really as broken up by the breakup as Priya said?

Stop obsessing, she told herself. *You did what you needed to do. You weren't trying to hurt Jordan. You weren't.*

Brynn logged on to the camp blog, hoping to find something to distract her from the Jordan situation, even if only for a few minutes.

Posted by: Priya
Subject: Friendship

I notice Brynn has some news she hasn't posted on the blog. She broke up with Jordan. I know, hard to believe, right? Since Jordan is awesome.

After the breakup, I started thinking about that post of Grace's. The one where she said what a good friend Natalie was because she had talked Brynn through a problem she was having. Now I'm thinking the problem Brynn was having was that she wanted to break up with Jordan. I have a question for all of you. Does a good friend really help somebody break up with a great guy? I'm just saying.

Brynn closed the blog without reading any of the responses. Right now, she didn't care what anybody but Jordan thought about their breakup. And she needed to know what he thought right now. She couldn't wait any longer. She was supposed to be at the theater for the first preview performance of *The Tempest* in three hours. That gave her more than enough time to make a detour.

Forty-five minutes later, she was walking up to Jordan's house. The bus had dropped her off two blocks away. Brynn wished it had been farther. She needed more time to figure out what to say.

She thought about walking away and doing a lap around the block. But it was too late. The front door was opening. And now Jordan was staring at her, his face blank. "Uh, can I come in?" Brynn asked. "I need to talk to you."

Jordan didn't say anything. But he took a step back and opened the door wider. Brynn hurried inside, still trying to figure out what to say. "I'm sorry," she told him. That seemed like a good place to start.

"For what?" Jordan asked as they stood face-to-face in the front hall.

"For . . ." Actually, good question. She wasn't really sorry she'd broken up with him. Not exactly, anyway. "For hurting you," she answered.

"You didn't," Jordan said.

"Priya told me—" Brynn began.

"Priya talked to you?" Jordan burst out. He didn't sound happy.

"Yeah. Well, she e-mailed," Brynn answered.

"She told me you were really upset."

"I'm not upset." He shoved his hands through his brown hair. "Look, you want to be with that Vern guy, then, whatever." Jordan shrugged.

"Wait. Back up. What about Vern?" Brynn asked.

"I know he's why you broke up with me," Jordan snapped. "Don't bother pretending he isn't. I saw the way you were always looking at him. And you were always talking about him all the time. Vern will think this. Vern will think that. And then you started having all those special little private rehearsals with Vern. I'm not an idiot, Brynn. Even if I can't recite Shakespeare like Vern."

Oh. So that's what Priya meant in her e-mail when she said Brynn should just get together with a drama boy. Priya and Jordan thought Brynn was breaking up with Jordan because of Vern.

"Vern is a complete jerk," Brynn explained. "I avoid Vern as much as I can. But I have to deal with him a lot. A ton of my scenes are with him. And since, by the way, my character is supposed to be in love with his character, I'm supposed to look at him that way. It's called acting."

"That one time I called you were at his house," Jordan accused.

"It was a place to rehearse. And I needed those extra rehearsals, even though I hated every second of them. Vern criticized the way I said every single word."

"If he's such a jerk, why do you care so much what he thinks?" Jordan demanded.

"Because Vern's a professional. He's been in commercials and he was on *Grey's Anatomy* once," Brynn explained. "He's doing what I want to do. That's why I broke up with you. Because acting is what I want to do with my life. This play is such a big chance for me. And I couldn't do my part the way I wanted to—the way I needed to—and still do girlfriend things with you."

Jordan gave a slow nod. "I guess I get that."

"It's not that I don't want to be your girlfriend. And it's so, so, *sooo* not that I want to be Vern's girlfriend." Brynn continued. "You're so great. No one makes me laugh as hard as you do. But I really can't hang out with you until after the play is over. It's going to take all my time doing so many performances a week and keeping up with all my school assignments. It just seemed like breaking up was the right thing to do."

"I don't really want to go months without seeing you. Forget about seeing. We haven't even been talking on the phone or IMing," Jordan said.

"And that's not going to change. At least not for a pretty long time," Brynn told him.

"I guess breaking up *is* what we should do," Jordan answered. He hesitated. "So you're really not going to start going out with that Vern guy?"

"Definitely not," Brynn promised. "He hates me as much as I hate him. And he never, ever makes me laugh."

Jordan smiled for the first time since Brynn had shown up.

"You don't hate me, too, do you?" Brynn asked him. She wouldn't be able to deal if he did.

Jordan shook his head. "Maybe this summer at camp . . ." He didn't finish the sentence.

"Would you want to . . ." Brynn couldn't finish her sentence, either. But she started to feel this crazy hope springing up inside her.

"It could be cool . . ." Jordan said.

"All those camp dances and everything . . ." Brynn said.

"Yeah, so, I'm definitely going to camp this summer," Jordan told her.

"Me too," Brynn answered. They stared at each other, and it was like they had this whole conversation without talking. A conversation where they agreed that this summer at camp they might try the whole boyfriend/girlfriend thing again.

"I guess you have to go," Jordan finally said. "The play . . ."

"Yeah, the play," Brynn agreed. "I do need to go."

"Good luck tonight," Jordan told her.

"Thanks. Thanks, Jordan." Brynn wanted to hug him. But she didn't think you were supposed to hug a boy you'd just broken up with.

"See you," Jordan said. He opened the door for Brynn.

"Bye." Brynn headed off. She felt both better and worse than when she'd arrived. Better because things were better with Jordan. And worse because things were better with Jordan. The way he'd acted had reminded her how cool he was. Brynn was going to miss him so much.

But there was always the summer. Maybe . . . .

She turned on to the street with the bus stop and almost smacked into Priya. This was perfect. Brynn really needed to talk to her.

"Hi! I was just over at Jordan's. We talked. He told me he thought I broke up with him because of Vern, which I so didn't," Brynn said, speaking so fast her words almost ran together. Priya was staring at Brynn like she was a slug that had ended up on the sidewalk.

Brynn rushed on. "I never would have broken up with Jordan for another guy. What other guy could be better than Jordan? No other guy, that's who. Especially not a conceited jerk like Vern. So, anyway, Jordan and I are all good. Or at least we're a lot better. He knows that I broke up with him because drama is so important to me. I need to give one thousand percent to the play, and that isn't fair to Jordan, because that means he gets zero percent."

She stopped to suck in a deep breath. "So are we good? Since Jordan and I are pretty good?"

Priya's eyes narrowed as she stared at Brynn. "No, we're not good. You broke up with Jordan over e-mail. I can't be friends with anyone who would do that. Even if you are smart enough to know Jordan's the best." She stepped around Brynn and strode away.

"Priya!" Brynn called after her.

But Priya rounded the corner without looking back.

▲ ▲ ▲

"Hurry. We're going to be late. And we can't be late," Natalie told Reed. She pulled him up the stairs to the roof of the Griffith Observatory.

"The stars aren't going anywhere," Reed told her.

"It's not the stars I'm worried about," Natalie answered, taking the steps two at a time.

Had her plan worked? Had Michael gotten Tori here? Natalie scanned the people taking in the view from the top of the observatory.

"Do you want to go into the telescope dome?" Reed asked, nodding toward the round tower with the copper roof off to their left. "The telescope in there is a lot better than the ones they put out on the roof."

"Do you see Michael around anywhere?" Natalie said, ignoring Reed's question.

"Michael? Why would Michael be here?" Reed raised his eyebrows.

"I asked him to try and get Tori here," Natalie admitted. "She and I had a massive fight yesterday. I didn't tell you about it because I didn't want to spoil our fun together, but now I just can't get the whole thing off my mind, so I figured she and I had to talk. But there's no way she would have agreed to meet me or even take my calls, probably. So I got Michael in on my plan."

"Why didn't you tell me your big plan?" Reed started looking around the rooftop, too.

"Do you ever have a thing that you think will get spoiled if you talk about it?" Natalie answered. "This felt like one of those things." She grabbed Reed's arm. "There they are. They haven't seen us yet." Michael was clearly looking for them, though.

"Well, we want them to see us, don't we?" Reed asked.

"Yeah, but let's get a little closer. I don't want to give Tori a chance to bolt before I can talk to her," Natalie answered.

"So she doesn't know why she's here?" Reed asked as they wove through the crowd toward Tori and Michael.

"Michael said there was no way she'd come if he told her. He also said if Tori kills him for tricking her into seeing me, that he'll come back and haunt me for the rest of my life," Natalie said. "Let's try and pretend that it's just a bizarre coincidence we're here at the same time."

"We can give it a shot," Reed told her. "You ready?"

Natalie nodded. She wasn't really ready. But she needed to do this. She hadn't been able to stop thinking about Tori.

"Michael, hey!" Reed called out.

Here we go, Natalie thought.

"Reed! What are you doing here?" Michael asked. He definitely should never try to go into acting. His voice came out way too loud and way too phony.

"Let's go," Tori said to Michael. "It suddenly stinks up here."

"Tor, don't leave," Natalie begged. "I know I got mad when we talked on the phone. But I really am sorry about what happened when we were supposed to meet up in Malibu. And the time I completely forgot we had decided to get together if my dad was busy."

"We'll be over there," Michael said, pointing to the opposite end of the rooftop. He and Reed walked off, like they couldn't wait to get away from Natalie and Tori and all their drama. Natalie didn't blame them.

"Come on, Tori. Talk to me," Natalie said.

"We were supposed to spend tons of time together while you were here. I canceled all my other plans. We were going to go to shopping at the Grove, and to Pink's for hot dogs, and that karaoke place in Koreatown. I told Michael I couldn't hang with him. And then you completely ignored me!" Tori cried. "Why should I want to talk to you? Go talk to Reed. You care more about him than you do me. Even though you just met him a few days ago. I guess you think boys are just more important than friends."

"I don't care more about Reed," Natalie protested. "He's not more important. At all."

"You've been spending every second with him. I saw the pictures of the two of you at the Ivy. And I'm sure you were with him earlier today. Am I right?" Tori demanded.

"Yeah," Natalie admitted.

"So you just drop your friends if a boy seems like he maybe likes you?" Tori asked.

"It's not like that. I swear," Natalie answered. "The day I went out with Reed when I was supposed to meet up with you, I was really upset. I'd hardly seen my dad at all, and I thought we were going to finally get to hang out together. Then he ended up having all this publicity stuff to do."

"You told me all that already. So you were upset. That's when you're supposed to be with your friends," Tori said. "Why didn't you call me?"

"Reed had left me a text message, and so I decided to call him up," Natalie said. "I just really wanted to talk to somebody who'd know how I was feeling. Your parents aren't divorced. You don't have to think about when you'll see one of them. You don't have to try and fit yourself into one of their schedules."

"I would have understood," Tori insisted.

"It's not the same as actually experiencing it yourself, though," Natalie said. "So Reed and I were talking, and that was cheering me up, so I asked him to hang out without even considering what you and I had talked about. I guess I was too upset by my dad to really think things through."

"Thinking about me," Tori cut in.

Natalie nodded. "I'm sorry, Tori. I really am. I just sort of forgot how sorry I was when I read what you wrote about me on the blog."

"You were right about that," Tori admitted. "I shouldn't have said all that in a blog post. I should have said it to your face if I was going to say it at all." She looked away from Natalie. "I'm sorry about that," she mumbled.

"And you get why I called Reed that day?" Natalie asked.

"I get why you called him. I still can't believe you forgot we had plans, though," Tori said.

"I can't, either. I was so psyched about all our plans. I went to Pink's today—"

"You went to Pink's without me?" Tori exclaimed.

"Well, you weren't speaking to me. And I wasn't

speaking to you," Natalie reminded her. "Anyway, you know how much I love those hot dogs. But I couldn't even finish one. My stomach was all knotted up because we'd had that horrible fight."

"It was pretty horrible, wasn't it?" Tori asked.

"Yeah," Natalie said. "Is it over?"

"It's over," Tori said, giving Natalie a quick hug.

"I still have a day and a half left. We can spend every second together!" Natalie told her.

"Including the Oscars!" Tori exclaimed. "I can't wait!"

The Oscars. Natalie's stomach started twisting itself into knots again. She'd given away Tori's ticket to the Academy Awards!

chapter

TWELVE

Natalie stepped over the tangle of cables in the hallway. "Dad?" she called.

"In here," he answered from his bedroom.

Natalie walked in and saw three camera people, a tall woman in a teal blue suit, a woman touching up everyone's makeup, and a guy doing a sound check. Who she didn't see was her father. "Um, Dad?" she called again.

"In the bathroom," he answered.

The bathroom door was open, so Natalie headed inside. "Madness, huh?" he asked. "The film crew is about to come in here and get some footage of me doing my pre-Oscar preparation. Good thing the bathroom holds twelve, right? The woman from ABC wants to interview me while I'm in a bubble bath. What do you think?"

"The guys who watch your macho action movies would probably faint," Natalie answered. "But your female fans would love it."

"So you vote yes?" her dad asked.

"As long as you make sure there are lots of bubbles," Natalie said.

Her father laughed. "Don't worry. I'll wear a bathing suit just in case there aren't."

The woman in the suit stuck her head in the bathroom. "Tad, do you think we could get some footage of you and your daughter? Maybe getting pedicures together?"

Natalie smirked. "You're getting a pedicure?"

"It's my special, special night," her dad joked. "You can get one, too, just not on camera." He turned to the anchorwoman. "I try to keep Natalie out of the public eye. Some paparazzi grabbed pictures of her the other night and they showed up all over the Net. I don't think she needs another dose of that right now."

"I guess that's my cue to leave," Natalie said.

"I'll send the manicurist down to you when I'm done," her father promised.

Natalie went to the kitchen and grabbed herself a bagel, then she returned to her room and logged on to the camp blog. Her friends had made her promise she'd give a moment-by-moment description of the whole Oscar day. She might as well post the first installment. But first she wanted to check the new messages.

Posted by: Brynn
Subject: My big bad

Well, you've all heard I broke up with Jordan. There's no such thing as a secret between the Camp Lakeview girls, right? So, I'm sure you also heard that I broke up with him by e-mail.

That was a bad, bad, stupid, stupid, mean, mean

thing to do. And I am hugely sorry. I hereby publicly apologize to Jordan, Camp Lakeview's best guy. I also apologize to Priya. (Although by apologizing to Jordan, I sort of did apologize to Priya. If you do something to Jordan, you do it to Priya. And vice-versa. That's how strong their friendship is. Which is pretty cool.)

In fact, I apologize to all of you. I messed up. I hurt people I care about. And I'm sorry.

Thanks for listening.

Brynn

P.S. Nat and Grace were there for me when I was trying to decide whether or not to break up with Jordan. I needed friends to help me think things through. But they didn't tell me what to do. And they definitely didn't tell me to do the breaking up through e-mail.

Posted by: Grace
Subject: Apology accepted

I forgive you, Brynn! (Not that you really need my forgiveness, but I forgive you anyway. Friends should always accept apologies. That's my philosophy. And you didn't even know I had a philosophy, did you?)

So how was the first performance of your play? I bet you rocked.

Grace

Posted by: Priya
Subject: Blame

Sorry I was throwing blame around about the breakup. Only one person sent that e-mail to Jordan.

P.

Posted by: Jenna
Subject: Apologies

My philosophy (hey, I have one, too!) is never apologize. It just makes you look guilty. Not that I ever need to apologize, anyway. As you all know, I am perfect in every way and never make mistakes.

Jenna

Joke of the day: Why don't wild dogs eat clowns? Because they taste funny.

Posted by: Valerie
Subject: Apologies

Jenna, you owe us all an apology for that clown joke!

Brynn, all of us mess up sometimes. You apologized, that's the important thing. (A-hem, Jenna.)

Now, B, tell us about your play!

Posted by: Brynn
Subject: The Tempest

The play went pretty well last night. There were a couple of technical difficulties. The lightning never lighteninged, for one thing. Plus the curtain got stuck halfway down at intermission and Prospero forgot to take his mic off, which led to the audience hearing some non-Shakespearean conversation from backstage for a minute. But I think I was pretty good. I didn't forget any of my lines, at least! And I didn't do anything I need to apologize for. (Anything new, I mean.)

I'll post the review of the play when it comes out. The theater critic for the *Boston Globe* is coming next weekend!

Posted by: Tori
Subject: More apologies

I have to give a mass apology, too. (And I hate to apologize. But I do it when I have to. Yes, I'm looking at you, Miss Jenna.)

I hereby apologize for my post screaming all that crud about Natalie. I was angry at her. And I had reason to be. But I should have shouted the crud at her face-to-face instead of on the group blog.

Nat—tell your dad good luck for me! I'll be watching at a friend's Oscar party with my fingers and toes crossed. Wait, I don't think I'll be able to cross my toes in the shoes I'm planning to wear. They are very pointy. The shoes, not my toes.

Natalie smiled as she read Tori's post. Tori was being so incredibly cool about the Academy Awards. She understood that Natalie couldn't just uninvite Reed because Tori and Nat had made up.

Natalie knew she'd have fun with Reed. But she also knew she'd have more fun with Tori. Reed wasn't going to be able to do a fashion evaluation of every celeb that walked down the red carpet. And the fashion was almost as big a part of the Oscars as the nominees.

Speaking of fashion . . . Natalie stood up. She

had to look at her dress one more time. She'd decided to go with one from Lulu's Dreamy line, pale blue tulle, fitted to the knees then flaring out, with feathers all around the bottom.

Whoops. She turned away from the closet and sat back down. She'd forgotten the whole reason she'd logged on to the blog. She was supposed to be describing Oscar Day.

Posted by: Natalie
Subject: bubbles

right this minute, my father is being interviewed while taking a bubble bath. this interview is for a news show! my father taking a bath is news. because it's part of his preparation for the oscar ceremony, and in hollywood everything about the oscars is newsworthy.

i will post again when the next oscar-related grooming and/or interview event occurs.

brynn, can't wait to read the review. you're going to be interviewed from your bathtub someday. i know it!

and priya, sometimes breaking up is the right thing to do, even with a really amazing guy. for example, logan's great, but i think we're better apart.

"The door was wide open and there were people coming in and out, so I just came on in myself."

Natalie jerked her head up and saw Tori standing in the doorway holding a garment bag.

"I'm so glad you came over! Are you going to help me get ready? I could use help. I'm more nervous about tonight than my dad is," Natalie said.

"You'll have to get yourself ready. I'll be busy getting myself beautiful," Tori teased.

"Huh?" It was all Natalie could think to say.

"Reed told me that I should go to the Oscars with you. Because I was your first choice and everything," Tori said. "Is that okay? Because if you want to go with Reed, I get it. Most people bring dates."

Natalie jumped up and gave Tori a hug. "You just made the best night so much bester!" Natalie exclaimed. "I've been wishing and wishing there was a way you could come with me. But I couldn't just disinvite Reed."

"Don't worry about Reed. He and Michael have an Oscar party to go to," Tori said.

"Perfect. I'm just writing a post for the camp blog. Give me one sec," Natalie told her. She started for the computer, then turned back toward Tori. "I am *sooo* psyched you're here."

guess what? tori just came in as i was typing this. she's going to be able to come to the oscars with me after all!! yay!!!

reed, the super nice and super cute boy i told you about, offered to give the ticket back to her. tickets to the oscars are like gold. reed's dad is alexander garrett, the big-deal director, and even he couldn't get tickets this year since he didn't have a movie nominated.

okay, more oscar-day news to come. tori and i are about to get our nails done. (pix to come.)

lawrence is going to do our hair. yep, that

lawrence, the one who did cameron diaz's hair in a beehive, complete with bees. i'm hoping there will be no insects involved in my 'do. but i guess you don't say no to lawrence, so . . .

bye for now.

natalie (and tori)

Just as Natalie was about to log off the computer, and IM popped up on her screen.

\<BicoastalBoy\>: Hey, Nat. Did you get my surprise yet?

\<NatalieNYC\>: yes! reed, that was so great of you. are you sure you're okay with missing the ceremony?

\<BicoastalBoy\>: I'm okay with missing the Oscars. Just wish I didn't have to miss your last night in town. You and Tori have fun.

\<NatalieNYC\>: you and i are going to see each other again. in ny or next time i'm here. or maybe our dads will do that movie together and we can meet on the set.

\<BicoastalBoy\>: We'll definitely see each other again sometime and someplace. Gotta go. Bye.

\<NatalieNYC\>: bye! i wish i could be in two places at once tonight. with you and with tori.

chapter

THIRTEEN

"I didn't know they closed this much of Hollywood Boulevard," Natalie said as she, her dad, and Tori headed for the Academy Awards ceremony. Bingley wasn't driving tonight. They were using one of the official limos hired for the Oscars. The traffic was crazy enough without trying to bring your own car.

"It's not just closed for tonight, either," her dad answered. "It's been closed for two weeks."

"Two weeks," Natalie repeated. "Why?"

"They have to put in the stadium seating for the fans. And they also do it for security," her father said. He looked out the window. "Okay, girls, it's almost go time. We're getting up to the red carpet. Stay close. I'm going to try to avoid most of the reporters. I'm talked out."

The limo pulled to a stop. The driver opened the door. Natalie's father stepped out first, and a huge cheer went up from the people who had been waiting for hours—or days—to get a spot where they could see the celebs arrive.

Natalie got out next, moving slowly to

keep her long dress where she wanted it to be. Not that anyone was watching her. The people in the crowd had figured out that she wasn't anybody they needed to look at, and were already trying to get a glimpse of the star who was in the next limo.

"This is insanely cool," Tori said as she and Natalie followed Nat's father up the red carpet. It was five hundred feet long. And every few feet there was somebody with a camera or a microphone.

Natalie's dad managed to avoid a lot of the interviewers—he only talked to about twenty on the way into the theater. But he didn't try to avoid his fans. He gave autographs to the people in the stands as he passed by them. Watching him made Natalie so proud.

"Look at the guy sweeping up trash," Tori said. "Even he's wearing a tux."

"Everyone who works the show has to wear a tux or an approved evening gown," Natalie told her.

"It almost seems like diamonds are required, too. Try and find a female star without a few," Tori said.

Natalie obediently glanced around. "I don't think Meryl Streep is wearing any."

"She's not exactly fashionable," Tori answered. "Oooh, look at the pink ones on that choker. I thought chokers were supposed to be out. But anything with pink diamonds is probably in."

"Uh-oh. Fashion disaster to the left," Natalie said softly. "The netting on those sleeves makes it look like she has some weird skin condition."

"It so does," Tori agreed.

This was so fun. Natalie and her friends always

did a fashion critique during the Oscars. But that was in front of the TV. Everything looked so much better—and so much worse—in person.

"It's freaky to be so dressed up when it isn't even dark yet," Tori commented, smoothing the fringe on the front of her emerald green flapper dress. She looked amazing. She had one of those thin jeweled bands around her forehead, like girls from the Roaring Twenties were always wearing in pictures. And she wore strands and strands of beads. A couple of them almost reached her waist.

"True," Natalie said. "But if they started the ceremony at eight thirty West Coast time, people on the East Coast would have to stay up until about three in the morning to see the whole show."

Tori moved closer to Natalie as they finally reached the entrance to the theater. "Shia LaBeouf just touched me," she whispered. "I don't think he meant to. I don't think he even knows he did. But I know."

"We're sitting in what they call the golden horseshoe," Natalie's father told Nat and Tori. "That's the semicircle of seats right in front of the stage. I'll get you girls settled, and then I'm going to get myself a drink from the bar. I didn't think I'd be this nervous. I'm actually sweating."

"You should have gotten botox in your pits, Mr. Maxwell," Tori told him. "That stops your body from producing sweat for a while."

"For some reason injecting cow toxins into my armpits doesn't seem like an entirely smart idea," he answered. "Here are our seats. I'll be back soon. Have fun."

"I'm the one who should have botoxed my pits," Natalie admitted. "I'm so nervous for my dad. This is his chance to prove to everybody he's a real actor, not just the action movie guy."

"He's going to win. I know it," Tori promised.

"I'm so glad Ellen is hosting again this year. I love her," Natalie said, looking around the theater—without looking like she was looking. She didn't want people to think she didn't belong. The place was huge. The plush red seats stretched back forever, and there were boxes rising up on both sides. Nat wondered who sat in them. All the nominees were up front with her.

Suddenly, there was a flurry of motion, with people moving down every aisle. "What's going on?" Tori asked.

"I think they're seat fillers," Natalie answered. "My dad told me the producers of the show don't want any empty seats to show up in front of the television cameras. So they have these people—just regular people—sit in the open seats. Like if someone leaves to go to the bathroom or get a drink."

"The show must be about to start, then," Tori said.

"I think so," Natalie answered. She twisted around in her seat, looking for her dad. He appeared just as one of the seat fillers started down their row toward his seat. "Sorry," her father told the guy in the tux. "This is my first nomination. I don't want to miss anything."

The guy grinned. "I don't blame you. I guess it's back to the holding room for me. Good luck!"

"What's the holding room?" Natalie asked her dad.

"Just a big room where the seat fillers wait when

they aren't needed. It's not a very exciting job," he answered.

"I'd do it," Tori said. "If I didn't have a friend with a big movie star father."

The lights in the theater dimmed, and Natalie felt like her whole body started to hum. She could hardly believe she was actually here. And that her dad had actually been nominated.

Natalie applauded as hard as she could when Ellen DeGeneres walked out onstage. She looked so small on that big, empty space. She wasn't alone for long. She'd barely gotten into her opening monologue when the stage was taken over by girls in Victorian dresses fighting alligators. A few moments later, a bunch of men with white canes joined the fight. Natalie figured they were supposed to represent her dad's movie, since the character he played was blind.

Her dad cracked up. It was kind of funny seeing all these characters from super-serious, classy movies battling it out over the giant Oscar statue in the middle of the stage. One of the Victorian ladies actually had one of the blind men in a headlock.

What felt like seconds later, it was already time for the first award to be presented. The night was going too fast. Natalie wanted it to last and last.

But she also wanted it to hurry up. The Best Actor Oscar was one of the last ones given out. She could hardly wait to see if her father had won.

She glanced over at him. He'd said he was nervous, but he didn't look it. Of course, he *was* an actor!

Ellen came out, told a few jokes, and then introduced Beyoncé. She was singing one of the Best Original Song nominees.

"Love her dress," Tori said in Natalie's ear.

Natalie nodded. Beyoncé was definitely on Natalie's personal Best Dressed list for the night. Her dress was very plain, but the color was anything but low-key. It was a deep orange that drew every eye. No one else had worn that color tonight. Blues and greens were the most popular. And of course, Tori was here in a green dress. She had fashion ESP. Lulu, too. She'd had lots of blues and greens in her collection, including the dress Natalie had gone with.

The night continued to whip by. More songs. More jokes. More envelopes being ripped open. More "and the Oscar goes to . . ." And then finally, Christina Ricci, last year's winner for Best Actress, took the stage. This was it. Last year's Best Actress always announced this year's Best Actor. This was the moment of truth.

"Here are the nominees for Best Actor," Christina said. Chills went up and down Natalie's spine. Christina listed the names of the other three actors, and then she said, "Tad Maxwell for *Dark Music*." Natalie grabbed her father's hand. Within three seconds they'd know if he'd won.

Tori grabbed Natalie's other hand. Natalie could feel the energy level go up in the room. Out in the rest of the country, Nat imagined every one of her friends holding their breath. Just the way she was holding hers.

Christina was opening the envelope now. Looking at the winner's name. *Say it, say it!* Natalie mentally urged. *Tad Maxwell. Tad Maxwell. TAD MAXWELL!!*

"And the Oscar goes to . . ." Christina paused. "Ty Conroy for *That One Night.*"

Natalie's father did a perfect job of smiling and applauding, even though she knew he had to be so disappointed. Natalie clapped and smiled, too. That's what you did at the Oscars. Even though her dad had given the best performance, and anyone with a tiny piece of brain should have known that and voted for him.

Her father leaned close. "It's an honor just to be nominated," he said in her ear as Ty Conroy began his acceptance speech.

Of course he had to say that. It's what every nominee, including her father, said in pretty much every interview leading up to the Academy Awards.

But she knew he was disappointed. He had to be. He'd wanted the Oscar so badly. He'd wanted to prove to everyone in Hollywood that he was a real actor.

▲ ▲ ▲

"As you from crimes would pardoned be, / Let your indulgence set me free."

The actor playing Prospero spoke the last lines of the play. As the stage faded to black and the curtain came down, Brynn felt the character of Miranda slip away from her for the night.

Her first Brynn-thought was about Priya. Why couldn't Priya accept her apology when Jordan had? She was angry at Brynn because of what Brynn did to Jordan. If Jordan was okay now, why couldn't Priya be okay, too? Tori and Natalie had had the huge, horrible fight, and they'd made up. They were out at some fabulous party right about now, having fun together. Why couldn't Priya hand out a little forgiveness?

The curtain came back up, and Brynn stepped forward with the other principals to take her bow. *Forget about Priya for now. Try and enjoy this moment*, she told herself as the applause swept over her. *You earned it. You sacrificed a ton to give the best performance you could in this play.*

The applause kept coming, so the cast took another step forward and bowed again. And that's when Brynn saw her. Priya.

She was about six rows back, and she was applauding harder than anyone. When she saw Brynn looking at her, Priya grinned. Then she threw a bouquet of roses toward the stage. Priya had a good arm—she was a total jock—so the roses landed right at Brynn's feet.

Brynn picked them up and hugged them to her chest, ignoring the little pricks from the thorns. "Thank you," she mouthed.

The second the curtain closed for the final time that night, Brynn rushed out to the lobby. Priya was there waiting for her. They stared at each other for a second, neither knowing what to say.

Then Brynn hugged Priya. "I'm so glad you came. I thought you were never going to speak to me again."

"I decided that Grace's philosophy was right," Priya said as Brynn released her. "If a friend apologizes, you should accept. I should have done that right away." She grinned. "I apologize."

Brynn grinned back. "I accept."

"Sorry you didn't win, Dad," Natalie said softly as they walked back down the red carpet together. Tori walked a few steps behind them. She could tell that Natalie and her father needed a little private time to talk. "I know how much you wanted it. But anyone who saw *Dark Music* knows you can really act."

He grinned at her. "You're right."

Natalie blinked in surprise. He sounded so cheerful. Of course, he was an actor. "Are you acting right now? Are you just pretending to be okay?"

"Martin Scorsese came up to congratulate me when I was at the bar. And P.T. Anderson. They both want to meet with me about projects. To be in movies directed by them, or Reed's father . . . Those guys don't work with you if you're not a real actor."

"And now they know you are. Because of *Dark Music*." Natalie smiled up at her father. "I'm so proud of you."

"You know what? I'm pretty proud of me, too." He wrapped his arm around her shoulders.

Nat's cell vibrated and she pulled it out of her tiny bag and checked it. "Aw, I just got a text message from Reed," she said over her shoulder. "He says my dad was robbed and he's going to write a letter to the Academy demanding an official recount," Natalie told Tori.

"He's a good guy. I approve of the two of you as a couple," Tori answered, stepping up next to Natalie.

"I approve of you as a couple, too. He has good taste. In actors and girls," Natalie's dad said.

"We're not a couple," Natalie protested. "I'm not ready to try the whole long-distance thing again. But we're going to try and see each other on one coast or the other sometime."

As soon as those words left her mouth, all Nat wanted to do was see Reed. Now—not sometime. True, they weren't a couple. But there was something between them. Something special.

"Our limo should be one of the first ones back," Natalie's dad said. "One of the perks of being a nominee. Even a losing nominee."

"You don't seem too sad," Tori commented.

"I'm an action movie guy who got nominated for an Academy Award," Natalie's father answered. "Most people didn't even realize I could speak a complete sentence until they saw *Dark Music*." He winked. "Besides, I won the People's Choice Award. That's the one that really means something because it comes from the fans."

"So you're okay? You're really okay?"

"I'm really okay," he told her.

If he was really okay, then . . .

"Dad—and Tori—would it be really horrible if I didn't want to go to the after-parties?" Natalie asked.

"The parties are the best part of the night. And we have invites to every single one," her father protested.

"But Reed, Natalie's non-boyfriend, doesn't," Tori explained. "And it's their last night together." She smiled at Nat. "It's okay with me if we just go to my place. Michael and Reed can meet us there." She turned to Natalie's dad. "If it's okay with you, too."

"Sure. I guess I can find somebody to talk to at the parties. Maybe one of the other losers." Natalie's father made an exaggerated sad face. Then he grinned.

"And maybe one of the winners will leave their Oscar lying around while they're dancing or something. I might get one after all."

"Try to get one for me, too," Natalie said. "I could give it to my friend Brynn."

"Will do," he promised. "That's our limo. You two take it. I can catch a ride."

It took about a half an hour to get off Hollywood Boulevard. But the rest of the drive to Tori's went fast.

"Did the guys sound like they minded leaving the party they were at?" Natalie asked as they got out of the car.

"They don't look too unhappy," Tori said. She gestured toward the open gate leading to the back patio. Natalie could see Reed and Michael lounging on deck chairs. Bags and bags from Pink's were on the flagstones between them.

Natalie ran over to Reed. She sat down next to him and grabbed the closest bag of hot dogs. "The food definitely isn't going to be anywhere near as good over at the Governor's Ball."

She pulled out a Guadalajara dog and took a big bite. It tasted delicious. Absolutely, completely delicious.

"We picked up a copy of your dad's movie from Blockbuster," Reed told her. "Michael and I thought we could all watch it together. It will totally prove that your father was robbed."

"Perfect," Tori said. "I loved that movie!"

Perfect, Natalie thought as Reed took her hand. The most perfect moment of the almost perfect night.

chapter

FOURTEEN

Brynn checked her e-mail before school on Monday morning. She hadn't gotten rid of the feeling that she needed to check it lots of times, even though things were fine with Jordan and Priya now.

From: imnotmichaelJORDAN
To: BrynnWins
Subject: Your play

Priya told me you were amazing in the play last night. She said it was like seeing a whole other person up there. I probably should have come, too. Sorry. It's just that the play is sort of why we broke up, and I just wasn't up for going. But I wanted to say congratulations. I know you worked really hard on your part.
Jordan

That was kind of . . . It kind of hurt to read Jordan's e-mail. Because it showed that even though he'd accepted her apology and everything, he was still kind of hurt. Hurt enough not to want to come see her in the play.

But things were already so much better between them than they had been a few days ago. And they'd keep getting better. Pretty soon, they'd be friends again, the way she and Priya were already back to being friends.

Then this summer . . . who knew?

She stared at Jordan's e-mail for another moment, trying to decide how to answer. She needed something friendly, but not girl-friendly. Something that would make Jordan think of the fun they always had together. Something that would make him think that she'd be someone he'd want to hang with this summer. Something that would make him know that she was still thinking about him . . . a lot.

From: BrynnWins
To: imnotmichaelJORDAN
Subject: Grotesque

I found a picture that's even grosser than the one you sent me two weeks ago. Try not to scream when you open it. Now you have to send me one back.

I totally get your not coming to the play. It's going to be running for a while. If you ever want to check it out, call or e-mail and I'll leave a ticket for you. Otherwise there are always all those dances at Camp Lakeview. Summer's going to be here faster than it seems.

Till then,

Brynn

Brynn nodded as she attached a photo of a turtle with two heads. It was such a Jordan kind of thing. She knew that—because they were friends. They'd always at least be friends.

▲ ▲ ▲

"I ate way too many hot dogs last night," Natalie said. "Try not to hit any bumps, Bingley. I might vomit."

"Oh, gross," Tori told her.

"Will do," Bingley promised. He got on the freeway. A green sign with a white plane pointed the way to the airport. Tori was riding with Natalie so they could have another hour or so together.

"Next time you come out, can we go to the the tar tar pits again?" Tori asked. "No one else will go with me."

"Definitely," Natalie answered. "But what about Michael? I thought you could make him do anything."

"Almost. He'll even go shopping with me. But he draws the line at the pits. He says the smell makes him sick," Tori said.

"We have to go see Kevin, the street Elvis, next time I'm here, too. Reed told me about him. We were going to go to the Baja Fresh on Hollywood and Vine where he performs, but then our dads ended up taking us to the Ivy instead."

"Oh, poor you," Tori crooned.

"I'll get my dad to take both of us there next time I'm here," Natalie promised.

Tori pulled a little notebook with a spangled

cover out of her purse. "I'm going to make a list. I don't want us to forget any of the stuff we want to do."

"We should make a New York list, too," Natalie said. "You have to come visit me there. We would have the most fabulous time. There's this place where—"

The ring of her cell interrupted her. Natalie smiled when she saw Reed's name on the screen. "Hello."

"What are your feelings about New Zealand?" Reed asked.

"I don't actually think I have any," Natalie confessed.

"It's supposed to be awesome. Let's go there sometime this summer. When you're not at camp," Reed said.

"Umm. I don't know about your parents, but mine—" Natalie began.

"Both our dads will be there. They just finalized the deal on that movie they wanted to do together. They'll be shooting there for months," Reed explained.

"Okay. Then I will see you in New Zealand," Natalie told him. "I've got to go. We're at the airport. But I'll call you from the best place in the world."

"The best place for pizza, anyway," Reed answered. "Bye."

Tori raised her eyebrows when Natalie hung up. "You're meeting Reed in New Zealand?"

"Our fathers are doing a movie together," Natalie said. Bingley opened the door for her. "I guess we'll have to finish our lists on the phone or IM."

Tori nodded. "See you at camp."

"See you at camp," Natalie agreed, giving Tori

a hug. She knew this summer they'd be better friends than ever. Fighting and making up and making plans did that.

Turn the page for a sneak preview of

camp
CONFIDENTIAL
Super Special!

Charmed Forces

chapter ONE

Posted by: Alyssa
Subject: Camp Preview—6th Division Rocks!

Hello all 6th Division Lakeview chickadees! School's out and it's time for camp. Just want to let you know that I have done my research and I have a STRONG feeling this is going to be the best summer ever! All signs point to yes!

And in case you're wondering how I know this, I had my first ever tarot card reading yesterday and Lady Gisela told me that camp is going to kick it this year. She also told me I'm seriously psychic! So I bought a book about new-age phemonoma and am busy gathering tools to help "bring my gift to the surface," as Lady Gisela says. Turns out a psychic needs a lot of stuff, like crystals, tarot cards, astrology books, tea leaves . . . I'm just getting started.

Here's what I know so far about the next three months:

Horoscope: "As Jupiter moves into Cancer and squares with Mercury, this summer is all about magic! Friendship, love, and nature play strong roles." Friendship, love, and nature? Sounds just like camp!

Ouija board: A friend of mine from school, Tally, slept over last night and we used the Ouija board. We asked the spirits what kind of summer we'll have. The spirits told Tally that she'll be fighting off a cold for most of July, but they told *me* that this summer will be full of sun and fun. Poor Tally—but yay us!

The *I Ching*:
Li/The Clinging, Fire
The Judgment: The Clinging.
Perseverance brings success.
Care of the cow brings good fortune.

Can't argue with that, can you? Maybe there will be a cow at camp we can take care of. Or something. OK, I don't really know which cow the *I Ching* is talking about, but whatever, trust me, it's good.

So buckle your seatbelts—it's going to be one for the record books! Can't wait to see you all on Sunday!

Love, Alyssa

Posted by: Natalie
Subject: Re: Camp Preview—6th Division Rocks!

you're psychic now? i guess that fits with the rest of your personality, your royal artsiness. but you forgot one great fortune-telling source—what did the magic 8 ball say?

xo nat

Posted by: Alyssa
Subject: Our Future

Hate to break it to you, Nat, but everyone knows the Magic 8 Ball doesn't really tell fortunes. It's a toy. But since I'm thorough, I checked it anyway. I asked, "Will this be the best summer ever for the 6th Division at Camp Lakeview?" Answer: "Reply hazy, try again." I tried again. This time the answer was: "Cannot predict now."

Which only proves my point: the Magic 8 Ball doesn't work.

"Just as I predicted," Alyssa said. "This summer is starting off right."

She stepped of the bus from Philadelphia onto sacred soil—Camp Lakeview soil. The camp grounds looked even better than last year, with fresh paint on the bunks and the lodge and the mess hall, the dirt paths newly swept and repaired, and even a sparkling new CAMP LAKEVIEW sign at the entrance.

Alyssa took another step and lost her footing. A small, round rock rolled under her foot and nearly tripped her. She bent down in front of the bus door and picked it up. Chelsea, who was getting off the bus behind Alyssa, bumped into her.

"Ohh!" Chelsea said. "Sorry, Alyssa." She wound her long blond hair into a knot on top of her head and popped her gum.

"Look at this!" Alyssa showed Chelsea a rock the size of a walnut, rough and mostly grayish brown, with a few glints of deep purple shining through.

Could it be an amethyst? Alyssa wondered. She had been looking for one. She'd read that amethysts promoted healing and psychic awareness, especially when touching the skin. They also helped people interpret dreams. They were practically magic! Every psychic should have one.

"So?" Chelsea said. "It's a rock. This place is crawling with them." She moved Alyssa aside so Natalie, Gaby, and Valerie could get off the bus. They all gathered around to see what Alyssa had found.

"It's not very pretty," Gaby said. "Except for that purplish part."

"I think it's an amethyst, and amethysts are very lucky," Alyssa said. "I'm going to go to the nature library and find out."

"I'm going to go to the kitchen and lock myself in the walk-in freezer," Chelsea said. "It's so hot!"

"Tell me about it." Gaby wiped the sweat off her forehead. "It's only June. I thought the mountains were supposed to be *cool.*"

"Maybe it will cool off tonight." Alyssa tossed her long black braid over her shoulder and hoisted her duffle bag. The girls started down the path to their bunk, 6A. Their division was still small, like last year, so all the Sixth Division girls would share one cabin.

The weather was unusually hot for the Poconos, but Alyssa didn't like to complain. She was fourteen now; this could be her last summer as a camper at Camp Lakeview and she was determined to enjoy it. Her parents had hinted that next year she might have to get a summer job.

As part of the camp's new look, each freshly-painted bunk had a different-color door: red, yellow, green, blue, orange, pink, turquoise . . .

"Look at the bunks!" Valerie said. "The doors have been painted new colors."

"I wonder what color door our bunk will have?" Natalie said.

"Care to make a prediction, O Mighty Alyssa?" Gaby said.

Before they reached 6A, Alyssa guessed, "Our door will be purple. In honor of the good-luck rock I just found."

She and Chelsea rounded the corner in the path at the same moment. Alyssa gasped. Natalie, Valerie, and Gaby gasped too.

"Oh my gosh," Natalie said. "Alyssa, you were right!"

There, nestled among the trees, stood their brown wooden cabin. The bright purple door had a white "6A" painted on it.

Alyssa rubbed the stone between her fingers. "Huh," she said. "I had a feeling about this thing."

"That was just a lucky guess," Chelsea said.

"Pretty lucky," Valerie said. "I never would have guessed purple."

The girls stepped inside their cabin. Alyssa dumped her duffle on a top bunk near the window. Natalie took the bunk below hers. The other girls began to settle in.

A tall, glamorous blond girl sat on a bunk, painting her toenails fuchsia.

"Tori!" Alyssa said.

Tori jumped to her feet. "You're here!" She hugged Alyssa and all the other girls, one by one.

"Where is everybody?" Alyssa asked.

Tori lay back down on her bunkbed, propping her feet on the wall and wiggling her fuchsia toes. "They were complaining about the heat, so Kerry took them down to the lake for a dip. They'll be back soon."

"Kerry's our new counselor?" Valerie asked.

"Uh-huh," Tori said. "She's nice, but she's not the kind of girl who understands the need for fresh toenail polish when you first get to camp—know what I mean? I had to do some talking to convince her to let me stay here and wait for you guys."

"We're glad you did," Gaby said as she began unpacking.

"It's so great to see you!" Natalie said.

"It's so great to see everybody!" Alyssa said. "But I have a little errand to do. I'll be back in a few minutes."

She hurried off to the nature cabin, clutching the rough stone. Why did she feel so attached to it already? So excited about it? Something about those glints of purple . . .

The nature cabin was quiet and deserted. Alyssa went to the library shelf and grabbed a book called *The Geologist's Handbook*. She paged through until she came to a picture of a rock that looked a lot like the one she'd found. There were two photos, sort of like "before" and "after" shots. The first picture showed a rough, grayish-brown rock with a slight grape tinge, like the one she held in her hand.

The other photo made her gasp.

It showed a glorious, gleaming cut and polished purple gem. An amethyst.

"I was right," Alyssa said to herself. The rock she'd found was an uncut, unpolished amethyst. Just what she needed to enhance her psychic powers.

Alyssa rubbed the amethyst happily. She was sure now that her predictions were right. This summer was going to be magic.